SAMSON

D1028444

ALSO BY TRACY A. MORGAN

Bathsheba: A Story of Sin and Redemption

SAMSON

TRACY A. MORGAN

Pacific Press® Publishing Association
Nampa, Idaho
Oshawa, Ontario, Canada
www.pacificpress.com

Cover design by Gerald Lee Monks
Cover illustration by Marcus Mashburn
Inside design by Aaron Troia

Copyright © 2010 by
Pacific Press® Publishing Association
Printed in the United States of America
All right reserved

Additional copies of this book may be obtained by calling toll-free
1-800-765-6955 or online at http://www.adventistbookcenter.com.

The author assumes responsibility for the accuracy of all facts and
quotations as cited in this book.

Library of Congress Cataloging-in-Publication Data:

Morgan, Tracy A.
  Samson / Tracy A. Morgan.
    p. cm.
  ISBN 13: 978-0-8163-2418-7 (pbk.)
  ISBN 10: 0-8163-2418-2 (pbk.)
  1. Samson (Biblical judge). 2. Bible. O.T.—History of Biblical events.
I. Title.
  PS3613.07485S26 2010
  813'.6—dc22

                                                        2010025619

10 11 12 13 14 • 5 4 3 2 1

DEDICATION

To my husband, Tim. Thank you for patiently coaching me through the "guy stuff" in this story. Every day you show me what real strength is. I love you!

A special thanks to Elsena Benson. You were so encouraging throughout the writing of this book. I appreciate the time you took to study with me and to give me feedback along the way. I'm so glad our paths crossed, even if it was only for a short time.

And to my mother-in-law, Iris Morgan. I can't thank you enough for all you do for our family. I know I don't say it enough, but I appreciate and love you more than words can express.

May God continue to bless each one of you.

Samson's Family Tree

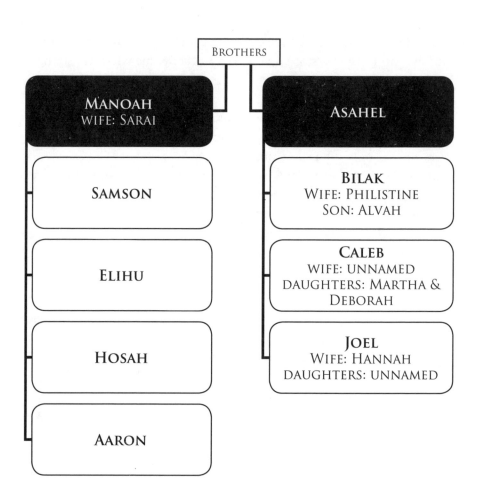

BROTHERS

MANOAH
WIFE: SARAI

ASAHEL

SAMSON

BILAK
WIFE: PHILISTINE
SON: ALVAH

ELIHU

CALEB
WIFE: UNNAMED
DAUGHTERS: MARTHA &
DEBORAH

HOSAH

JOEL
WIFE: HANNAH
DAUGHTERS: UNNAMED

AARON

CHARACTERS

Starred characters are biblical; all others are fictional.

*Samson	Nazirite judge of Israel
Sarai	Samson's mother
*Manoah	Samson's father
Elihu and Hosah	Samson's twin brothers (four years younger than Samson)
Aaron	Samson's youngest brother (eight years younger)
Asahel	Samson's uncle (Manoah's older brother)
Joel	Samson's cousin (Asahel's youngest son); former soldier
Hannah	Joel's wife
Caleb	Samson's cousin (Asahel's middle son)
Bilak	Samson's cousin, who was killed by the Philistines (Asahel's oldest son)
Alvah	Samson's half-Philistine cousin (Bilak's son)
Martha	Samson's cousin (Caleb's older daughter)
Deborah	Samson's cousin (Caleb's younger daughter)
Peles	Samson's Philistine wife from Timnah
Metsor	Peles's younger sister
Phicol	Peles's father
Saph	young Philistine man from Ashkelon
*Eli	high priest in Shiloh
*Delilah	Samson's mistress from the Valley of Sorek
Jachin	prisoner in Gaza
Maoch	Philistine lord of Gaza
Danites	Samson's tribe

Simeon	Old man whom Samson pulled out of the Philistine jail
Abihu, Elam, Terah, and Gehazi	prisoners in Gaza

PLACES

Zorah	Samson's birthplace on the foothills overlooking the Sorek Valley
Mahaneh-dan	"Camp of Dan," 2.5 miles northeast of Zorah (west of Eshtaol)
Timnah	Philistine town 4 miles northwest of Zorah
Shiloh	one day north of Mahaneh-dan and spiritual capital of Israel during the time of Judges
Ashkelon	Philistine state on the coast where Samson killed 30 men and took their clothes
Etam (Rock of)	Site of the famous "jawbone" battle, just south of Bethlehem
Lehi	Judean town near the Rock of Etam
Gaza	Philistine state in the south, place of Samson's death
Gath	Philistine state in the north
Ramah	village of the Negev
Beersheba	where Joel met his wife, Hannah
Hebron	Hilltop town where Samson searches for Joel
Eshtaol	near Zorah, where Samson is buried
Sorek Valley	Delilah's home

· PART 1 ·

CHAPTER 1

Samson floated in and out of consciousness in what seemed to be a nightmare that wouldn't end. His body burned with pain as he felt himself being dragged across the ground. But that pain was minor compared to the rhythmic pounding that threatened to explode his head. When Samson refused to walk, he was thrown over the back of a horse and jostled roughly along. At one point, he slid off the horse and lay on sharp rocks until someone stopped to pick him up. He prayed for death, but instead he was engulfed in a throbbing darkness that threatened to overcome him.

His agony didn't allow him to even try to keep track of where he was going or how much time had passed. He knew when he was being paraded through a Philistine town, because he could hear the insults being hurled at him, and he could feel the spit and kicks landing on him from time to time. Twice he was given a bitter drink that eased his pain momentarily; sometimes he was given a hard piece of bread to chew on, but he never felt hungry or thirsty—all he felt was an excruciating throbbing in his head and face. Then the fever began, bringing delusions with it. The Philistines must have thought he was going to die, because they stopped in what smelled like a seaside town and laid Samson on some moldy hay to rest. When the jostling finally stopped, his pain eased and he fell into a restless sleep.

In the constant darkness around him, he could hear voices. They were usually the rough grunts of the soldiers, but sometimes the voice of a woman hung close to his face. He wasn't sure if she was real, and he didn't care. As he drifted between consciousness and sleep, the woman's voice changed. Sometimes it sounded like Delilah, seductively cooing in his ear. Sometimes it sounded like his wife, Peles, screaming from the flames of her father's house. But usually, the voice sounded like his mother. He somehow knew she wasn't really there, but it was comforting to imagine she was. The fever turned the rough efficient hands that dressed his wounds and poured liquid down his throat into the gentle hands of a mother caring for her sick child. He hoped he would wake up and find himself in his parents' home in the hills of Zorah.

The fever overcame him once again, and he faded back into a dream-filled sleep.

* * * * *

"Tell me the story again," Samson begged as he lay on his stomach with his chin propped on both hands and his feet bouncing restlessly at the end of gangly legs.

"Aren't you tired of this story yet?" his mother asked as she helped her younger sons get ready for bed.

"Yeah, story, story!" little Elihu exclaimed as he wiggled out of the short goat-hair robe that covered his undergarments.

"Please!" begged his twin brother, Hosah.

"Oh all right," Sarai sighed playfully. "Let me see if I remember it." She smiled and pretended to think hard. All three of the boys lay down on their mats, listening attentively.

"Well, I was drawing water from the cistern, and your father was out grazing the herd, when all of a sudden, I felt as if someone or something was standing right behind me."

"Was it a lion?" Hosah asked.

"A bear?" Elihu joined in.

"A Philistine soldier?" Samson played along.

"No, it was a man. But He wasn't an ordinary man. I could tell right away there was something unusual about Him."

"How could you tell?" Samson asked, already knowing the answer.

"It's hard to explain, but He was dressed so beautifully, and He seemed to be glowing. I can't tell you why, but as soon as I saw Him, I fell to my knees and hid my face from Him. Then He spoke—and it was like lightning had hit the ground nearby. All the little hairs on my arms and on the back of my neck stood up, and my heart was pounding so hard in my chest that I thought I would die."

"What did He say?" the twins asked at the same time.

"He told me my prayers had been heard and that I was going to have a son. You see, I wanted a baby more than anything else in the entire world, but I was already getting too old. You boys will understand when you are older, but do you see the gray streaks in my hair?" Sarai loosened a strand of hair from under the veil that covered her head. "Women with gray hair like mine usually have grandchildren—not babies of their own." She smiled to herself as she was pulled back into the memory. "The Man told me my son would be a Nazirite."

Samson sat up on his mat and smiled. This was his favorite part of the story.

"I had heard the term before, but I really didn't know what a Nazirite was, so I asked the Man what it meant. He told me that the boy could never get his hair cut or touch a dead body. He also couldn't eat unclean foods or anything from the vine."

"Like grapes!" Elihu said, obviously pleased with himself.

"Yes, darling, like grapes." Sarai smiled at her smallest son and continued. "The Man told me I had to follow the same rules while the baby was inside of me so that he would be set apart right from the very beginning of his life."

"Set apart for what, Mother?" Samson asked, looking more serious now.

"The boy is special," she answered, looking straight into the eyes of her oldest child, wondering if she should tell him the rest of the story yet.

"Then what happened?" Hosah asked, breaking the spell that fixed Sarai's eyes on Samson.

She took a deep breath and then continued. "Well, I wanted to tell your father right away, so I ran down the hill, into the valley, and I found him there with the sheep and goats. I told him everything that had happened, and we prayed right there that the Man would come back."

"The Man did come back, didn't He?" Samson asked.

"Yes, He came back. It was a few days later. I was working in the field, pulling weeds, and there He was. This time I asked Him to stay so I could get my husband. I should have offered Him some food, or at least a place to rest, but I was so excited I just left Him standing right there in the garden! I quickly found your father and brought him to the Stranger who, thank God, was still right where I had left Him. After He explained everything to us again, about how to raise the boy, your father invited Him to eat with us. The Man said He didn't want to eat but that we should offer a sacrifice to God instead."

Sarai had all three of the boys' complete attention now.

"So, Father selected a young goat and some grain to offer as a sacrifice, and he put it on the altar."

"The one near the house?" Elihu asked.

"That's right. The same altar we use for all of our family sacrifices when we're at home."

"Then what happened?" the ever-curious Elihu asked for the tenth time that day.

"Before your father could light the offering, a flame came out of the cold stone altar and flashed up toward the sky. It was a huge fire that burned as high as I could see." She leaned closer to her children and spoke so softly that her voice was almost a whisper. "Then the most amazing thing happened."

"What?" all three boys gasped.

"The Man rose up off the ground—right into the flame, but He didn't burn up. Then He rose up into the sky until we couldn't see Him anymore."

"What was His name?" Samson whispered.

"He wouldn't tell us His name. He said it was too wonderful for us to understand."

Without further explanation from their mother, all three boys nodded. Even the young twins understood that the Lord Himself had visited their parents.

Sarai kissed the twins on the head and pulled a large goat-hair blanket over them. Then she knelt next to her oldest son, Samson, and held both of his hands in hers.

"Good night, my precious Nazirite," she said as she brushed his long hair from his forehead with her fingertips. "May God continue to watch over you and bless you." She kissed him softly and left the room.

CHAPTER 2

"Samson, sit still. Why are you so fidgety this morning?" Sarai chided as she brushed the boy's long hair back from his face and tied it with a leather thong.

Every morning for weeks, Samson had awakened early and waited for the word from his father that he could help graze the flocks. He had caught bits and pieces of conversations between his parents, and he knew it would be soon.

His father approached the fire and sat down to join his wife and son for breakfast. Samson thought he caught a quick, secretive smile that was meant for his mother's eyes only.

"Father, may I go with you today? Please! I'll listen to everything you say, and I'll be very helpful," Samson begged.

"I don't know, son. It's very hard work looking after sheep and goats all day. You're still practically a baby."

"I'm not a baby!" Samson exclaimed, feeling very offended. "I'm almost nine years old!"

His father chuckled. "You're hardly even eight."

"Well, I'll be nine someday!" Samson muttered under his breath.

"He's young, but he's big for his age, and he is very helpful. Perhaps he won't be much trouble for you," his mother played along.

"Yes, but he's so much help to you here. He looks after his two little brothers, and now that we have another baby on the way, I'm sure you could use him here at the house," Father replied.

"That is true, but I think I can handle the little ones today." As if on cue, Samson's four-year-old twin brothers burst out of the house and ran to the eating area outside. They seemed to bring noise and chaos with them wherever they went.

"Breakfast!" Elihu yelled as his twin bumped into him and knocked him to the ground.

Manoah scooped up the two boys and sat them on their mats while Sarai served everyone food.

Samson tried to eat, but it was difficult to swallow anything. Even the possibility of joining his father at work was far too exciting for him.

"Well, Samson, I suppose if you want to come with me today, you may," Manoah said casually. But before he could finish, Samson was on his feet, jumping up and down.

"But first, you finish breakfast." Sarai gently put a hand on his shoulder and sat him back down.

Samson managed to eat everything that was put in front of him. He waited patiently while his mother packed lunches and filled skins with goat's milk for him and juice for his father. Samson knew without asking that he could not have juice or any of the other foods and drinks made from grapes. His parents told him how God had chosen him to be a Nazirite, and he understood that it was just part of life for him. Even though he lived in a region that was known for its vineyards and wine, Samson would never dream of breaking the vow that his parents had made with God.

At last, Manoah called for him to help lead the animals out of their enclosure. Samson watched every move and listened to every word his father told him. He knew if he did well, he would be allowed to come again; but if he didn't, he was stuck at the house with his mother and little brothers.

Samson walked beside his father as the herd reached a stream. The youngest animals were nudged closer to the water by their mothers so they could drink. Manoah was alert to any potential predators that might attack his animals. His flock was still considered small, but it had grown substantially in the few short years since Samson was born. Every spring new lambs and kids were born healthy and strong; and thanks to Manoah's watchful eye, very few were injured or killed.

"We must be careful here at the water, son. Many predators would be happy to snatch a lamb if given the chance. My old eyes aren't what they used to be, so I'm counting on you to watch for danger."

Samson's eyes scanned the horizon. He could see the villages far off in the distance of the valley. He could see a few houses, including his own, dotting the hillsides. Out of the corner of his eye, he thought he caught a glimpse of something scampering behind a rock. He watched carefully until he saw it again. Sure enough, it was a pair of small gray dogs with long, bushy tails.

"Father, jackals!"

"Ah, yes, they're everywhere. They will sometimes take young lambs if they stray from their mothers. But it's the bigger predators that we have to watch for. This valley is known to have lions and bears lurking around. If you see them before they get too close, you can sling rocks at them. Often they'll leave to find easier prey." He unhooked his sling from his girdle and demonstrated for his son. "I used to be pretty good with this. Let's see . . . just put a stone in here like this, twirl it, and release it underhand." Samson watched as his father's rock landed with a thud several yards away. "Here, you give it a try," Manoah said as he handed the sling and a smooth stone to his son.

Samson did exactly what his father had done, but he aimed for the small head of the gray jackal that peeked out from behind a rock off in the distance. He swung the sling and released the stone. To his surprise, he heard the jackal yelp. "Oh! Did I hit it?" he exclaimed.

"I guess you did!" his father replied, looking just as shocked. "Here, give it another try." He scooped up another stone and handed it to his son.

"I'll try to hit them again," Samson said as he aimed for the two jackals that were now running away.

"Well, hitting a moving target from that distance is almost impossible. Try for something easier . . ." Manoah's words trailed off when he heard a second yelp.

Both man and boy stood in shock for a moment. Samson was too young to realize that it was nothing short of supernatural, but Manoah knew better. In the years that had passed since Samson's birth, somehow he had almost forgotten that the boy was destined to do great things. This sudden reminder filled Manoah with an unexplainable mixture of pride and fear for his son's future. Manoah had lived his entire life under the thumb of the Philistines. He had seen firsthand what they did to those who tried to stand up to them. The message delivered years earlier by an angel was now becoming a reality. The fact that his boy was destined to stand before the Philistines on behalf of all God's children hit Manoah as hard as the stone had hit the jackal.

Samson stood a little taller when he recognized the pleasure he initially saw reflected in his father's eyes, but then a dark shadow passed that the boy could not understand. For the first time in his young life, he saw real fear in his father's eyes.

CHAPTER 3

Samson's concerns about not pleasing his father were soon erased when he was given more responsibilities every day. Each morning he continued to help his mother milk the shaggy black doe goats. Once that task was complete, Sarai took the milk and poured it into skins to make butter, cheese, and yogurt. While Sarai took care of the food, Samson and his little brothers were sent outside with baskets to pick up sticks and animal droppings that could be dried in the sun and used for the fire. It was a dirty, smelly job, but nothing went to waste, and everyone had to help out. After everyone had washed and eaten breakfast together, Samson and his father would begin the task of caring for the flock. Manoah whittled a shepherd's staff for Samson out of a large terebinth branch. It was Samson's most prized possession, and he always stood a little taller when he carried it. Manoah showed his son how to hold the staff over the small opening of the animal enclosure. As the sheep and goats passed under the staff, they were counted. If any animals needed to be coaxed out of the pen, the staff could be used to direct them toward the opening. Once all of the sheep and goats where accounted for, Manoah led them toward the greenest pastures, which varied depending on the season.

As the spring days grew longer and warmer, Manoah told Samson it was time to shear the sheep. Samson was thrilled to try something new. He watched silently while his father lifted one of the calmer ewes and laid her over his lap. He spoke softly to her while his hands quickly and efficiently cut the thick wool from her body in one single piece. When he was finished, he released her, and she trotted off, shaking like a wet dog. He sent Samson to grab another ewe, and this time the boy held her while his father expertly clipped the wool.

One by one, all the docile sheep were sheared until only the large ram remained. Samson had nicknamed him Ra (the Hebrew word for *evil*) after being chased and pushed around by the animal a few too many times. Samson saw how tired his father had become, so he bravely volunteered to catch the beast. The animal enclosure was butted up against the side of the hill with a small cave carved out of the limestone wall. The sheep and goats often went into the cave to escape storms, but they generally came out when they were called. Ra saw what was happening, and he quickly escaped into the cave when it was his turn. Samson stepped into the darkness of the cave and waited a moment for his eyes to adjust. As he walked farther from the sun-filled opening, a chill ran down his spine, and he suddenly became frightened of the blackness that surrounded him. He realized he had never been in such complete darkness before. At night, his mother always kept a lamp burning in the house. Every Hebrew woman did. The light inside told anyone passing by that the house had a family living in it. Even the poorest homes had lamps burning. For the first time in his life, Samson was without the comforting glow of light. The last thing in the world he wanted to do was disappoint his father, so with his staff in his hand, he stepped farther into the cave, calling softly for the ram. He heard the click of the animal's hooves on the limestone floor, and he turned toward the sound. "Come on, Ra, don't be difficult," he whispered. "It's just a little haircut, nothing to get worked up over." The hooves clicked closer this time, and Samson leapt forward, hitting nothing but the ground. He picked himself up and stood very still, listening. Suddenly, he heard the animal coming straight for him. He ran away from the sound, but it was too late; Ra hit him in the back with his large curved horns. Samson quickly turned and tried to grab hold of the animal, but Ra shook him off.

"Are you all right in there, Samson?" he heard his father call from outside.

"Yes, I'll get him." He desperately wanted to prove himself to his father.

Samson took a deep breath, trying to listen past the pounding of his heart. "God, help me be brave," he whispered aloud. Then he heard it, a soft snort just a few steps away. Softly, he walked toward the sound with his right hand on his staff and his left hand reaching out in front of him like a blind man might feel his way. His staff bumped against the ram, causing him to charge toward Samson again, but this time the boy was ready for him. He tossed his staff onto the ground and with both hands grabbed the ram's horns pulling him toward the opening of the cave. He pulled and tugged, walking backward into the bright sunshine, where his father waited, a huge smile on his face.

"Well done, boy!" Manoah exclaimed when he saw the pair locked together. "Now bring him over here and wrestle him to the ground for me."

Samson twisted the ram's horns to the left, and the animal's body moved in the same direction. After a bit more twisting and pulling, Samson was able to get Ra on his side. "Lie down on top of him and hold him steady," Manoah instructed his son as he rushed over with his tools in hand. Ra kicked and bleated for a few more minutes, but he finally realized he was beaten. At last he lay still, and Samson could hold him with hands placed at the shoulder and hindquarters. Manoah was then able to move in and shear the wool.

"When I count to three, you quickly back away, so Ra doesn't hurt you," Manoah instructed his son. "Ready? One, two, three!"

Samson jumped up, but the ram stood to his feet, shook himself, and trotted off.

"Well, I think you've tamed the beast, my boy!" Manoah exclaimed as he slapped his son on the back. "Let's get this wool put away and get some rest. Tomorrow we start our next adventure. We'll take the herd to graze on my brother's land in Mahaneh-dan and then set off to Eshtaol to sell our wool."

"You mean I get to go with you?"

"Of course you do. I'm getting too old to do this job alone. You've proven yourself to be a very valuable help to me. Now go get your staff and get cleaned up for dinner."

The compliment made Samson beam. He didn't even mind going back into the blackness for his staff. Once inside, he looked up at the dark ceiling and whispered, "Thank You, God! I know You're always with me."

CHAPTER 4

Samson was so excited, he didn't expect to get much sleep, but fortunately his battle with the ram was enough to exhaust both his body and mind. It seemed like only minutes until Samson's father gently shook him awake.

"Samson, it's time. Don't wake your brothers."

The sun wasn't even up yet, but his mother and father were already busy making preparations for the short trip to Mahaneh-dan. Manoah had packed the wool into a simple wooden cart that could be pushed or pulled, depending on the terrain. The cart was completely full, so Samson and Manoah would have to carry packs on their backs filled with food and other supplies. After a quick breakfast, they said their goodbyes to Sarai and moved the herd in the direction of the rising sun.

"If we hurry, we'll get to my brother's house in time to help him with the shearing," Manoah said as he grunted against the weight of the cart and the pack on his back. "He has a much larger flock than we do, so he can use the extra hands. He'll be so surprised to see us. He won't believe how much you can do now!" He stopped to catch his breath.

Samson tried to be helpful by pushing the cart from behind, but it was difficult to direct the animals and handle the load at the same time. He had to remind himself that it was a short trip, and, after the compliment his father had just given him, he wasn't about to complain.

It didn't take long for the small caravan to reach the valley, where the ground was less rocky. The sheep stopped to graze on the soft grass. The goats quickly tired of the grass and wandered around nibbling on low branches or anything else they could find. The Sorek Valley was a lush, fertile area with a cool, clear stream running from the northeastern hills of Ramah into the Great Sea in the west.

CHAPTER 4

Though Samson hadn't done much traveling in his few short years, he was sure the lands given to his tribe, the Danites, had to be the best in all of the Promised Land. Unfortunately, the Philistines who lived in this part of the country had no intentions of leaving—even though God had given the land to the Israelites. Samson had heard his father talk many times about the Israelites entering the Promised Land after God had led them out of Egypt and through the desert for forty years. If only they would have obeyed God and cleared the land of all the pagan enemies and their false gods. But now, they lived right next door to them.

Some of the Israelites had married Philistines and had even begun worshiping their gods. No wonder Yahweh, the true God of heaven, let the Philistines rule over them. What else could He do? Samson hoped someday God would answer the prayers of the people who were still faithful to Him. Maybe soon He would send a deliverer.

After allowing the animals to eat their fill, Samson and Manoah moved the herd on. The caravan reached the small town of Mahaneh-dan well before the sun was high overhead. Samson had been to his uncle's house many times to celebrate holidays, but this was the first time he was participating in the shearing. During past visits, there had been relatives outside greeting them, but today the streets were practically empty. With the exception of a few old women and small children wandering around, the town seemed to be deserted. Manoah led Samson and his animals to the edge of the village, where the townspeople had gathered for the sheep shearing. Every able-bodied man, woman, and child in Mahaneh-dan was there, working together to get the job done. To Samson, it looked like chaos at first, but then as he watched, he realized everyone had an important role. Boys worked with the men to catch and hold down the sheep while their thick winter coats were removed. The women stacked the fleece neatly in separate piles for each family. Girls drew water from the well and carried it to large troughs for the animals to drink. Even the youngest children were kept busy brushing the fleeces to remove sticks and burrs. Somehow everyone just seemed to know what part they were to play in this drama that took place every year.

Manoah watched with a satisfied smile on his face.

"Why did you leave Mahaneh-dan?" Samson asked his father. "Don't you like being here with your brother and the rest of the family?"

"Of course I do, son, but our home is in the hills, away from the troubles of town living."

"How did you end up leaving your family and living in Zorah?" Samson asked.

"I left home when I was a young man to find a wife from our tribe. I met your mother and realized I didn't need anything else in this world to make me happy. Her father gave me a job and treated me like his own son. Since he had no male descendants, he left everything to me when he died." Manoah looked seriously at his son for a moment. "When you decide to marry, I hope you remember that you are choosing more than just a wife. The girl you marry will bring with her a family and a lifetime of happiness . . . or sorrow, if you're not careful."

Samson didn't really understand what his father was saying, but he nodded in agreement to please him.

Just then an old woman whom Samson knew only as "Auntie" noticed them standing at the edge of all the activities.

"Our Manoah is home!" she exclaimed over the noise.

"Brother!" Uncle Asahel released the ewe he was holding and ran to greet his guests. "What are you doing here? How is it you already have shorn sheep?" He glanced at the small herd that was restlessly mixing in with the other animals. "Did you hire someone to shear them for you? Why didn't you bring them to us as you always do?"

Manoah kissed his brother on both cheeks. "No, I did not hire anyone! My son helped me." Everyone nearby turned their attention to Samson.

"Who is this young man?" Uncle Asahel said as he tousled Samson's hair. "What has happened to your little boy?"

"I'm not little; I'm almost nine!" Samson replied without thinking.

Everyone nearby chuckled, and Samson blushed a deep red.

"Well then, young man, won't you come help us with our sheep?" Uncle Asahel said to Samson as he led him into the middle of the shearing activities. "It's a man's job, but you look like you can handle it!"

Samson jumped right in and worked as hard as he could. Knowing his father and uncle were watching was all the incentive he needed to do a good job.

CHAPTER 5

After the last of the sheep had been sheared and everything was cleaned up, the women hustled back to their homes to prepare a feast. The atmosphere changed instantly from one of hard work to celebration. Several people gathered around and greeted Manoah and Samson. The children who were no longer preoccupied with their duties now focused their attention on the new boy.

Samson knew his long hair was a source of interest for them, but he was always embarrassed by their open stares and whispers. As he counted the last of this father's sheep and made sure they were safe inside the enclosure with the rest of the animals, he felt someone tug on his hair. He quickly turned around to find a cluster of girls giggling. He knew immediately that his cousin Martha was responsible. She was only a year older than Samson, but she acted like she felt far superior. Every time Samson came to visit, she always made a point of teasing him, usually in front of her friends. Samson had spent many holidays teetering between trying to avoid the girl and trying to win her approval. This time, he was feeling especially brave after all the work he had just completed, so he tried a different approach with her.

"When are you going to grow up, Martha?" he asked her, trying to sound older. "I have long hair, and I can't drink grape juice. Big deal! Can't you find something better to do than tease me about it every time I come to town?"

Martha looked completely shocked, and her friends' giggles changed direction.

"Oh, Samson thinks he's a big shot now that he gets to help with the shearing," she retorted, obviously trying to redirect everyone's attention. "But I still think he looks like a baby. Samson's a long-haired, milk-drinking baby," she sang.

"I'm not a baby!" he exclaimed, blinking back tears. *So much for acting older,* he thought to himself as he marched off to find his father. He didn't notice a small girl chasing after him. It was Martha's little sister, Deborah.

"Wait, Samson. I don't think you're a baby," she said as she caught up to him and took his hand. "And I think you have pretty hair."

"Oh, what do you know?" he said roughly as he shook his hand free. When he saw the hurt look in her eyes, he quickly changed his mind and let her hold his hand. But Samson did peek over his shoulder first to make sure none of the older girls saw him.

When they approached Uncle Asahel's house, a crowd had already begun to gather. Deborah ran off to find her mother, and Samson looked for his father. He quickly found him talking to Uncle Asahel about something that seemed serious. When they saw him approach, they turned their attention toward him. Samson had the feeling they had been talking about him.

"There's our young Nazirite," Uncle Asahel said as he put his hand on the boy's shoulder. "Your father tells me you are turning into quite the shepherd, but tending sheep won't help you kill Philistines."

Samson didn't know what to say. *Why would I kill Philistines?*

"Now, brother, leave him alone. He's just a boy," his father jumped in quickly.

"Yes, but he is very big—and strong. I'd say it's about time for him to start training."

"Training for what?" Samson asked, feeling thoroughly confused.

"Don't rush him; he's too young. Besides, perhaps he's not meant to be a military leader. We don't know what God has planned for him yet," Manoah replied, as though Samson weren't even there.

"My son Joel can teach him many things," Asahel continued, with his hand still on Samson's shoulder. "There's no point wasting all his military training just because he's decided he'd rather stay home and hide away with his wife and baby. If he's not willing to go out and fight the Philistines himself, he can at least share what he knows with Samson. How else are you going to know what skills the boy has? He needs to begin his training now. Leave him with us this summer. The sheep are sheared; you will manage without him."

"I'm not like you, brother. I'm not eager to see my son prove his bravery on the battlefield. You should be able to understand that; you lost your oldest son to the Philistines. Don't ask me to endanger my firstborn."

"I'm not the one asking you, Manoah." Samson was surprised to hear the sharp edge in his uncle's voice. "How can you doubt God Himself?"

CHAPTER 6

That evening, Samson sat around the fire with his family, still puzzling over the conversation between his father and uncle. Why would he need military training? Would his father really leave him in Mahaneh-dan? Fortunately, the smell of the food made him forget his concerns—at least for the time being.

The wine flowed freely, and heaping trays of meat, bread, vegetables, and fruits were passed around. Samson devoured his food with an appetite that more than one family member commented on. There were also plenty of remarks about the foods Samson chose to avoid. When an aunt served him a steaming piece of pink meat, he shot his father a questioning look.

"Oh thank you, Auntie, but Samson does not eat pork. Remember, he is a Nazirite," Manoah politely said as he took the meat off of Samson's plate.

"Yes, but it's good meat," she replied, looking offended. "A Philistine woman in Eshtaol taught me how to cook it just right. Let him try a little. Can't you see he's hungry?"

"Aren't you an Israelite?" Samson asked innocently.

For a moment, everyone was silent. Finally, the aunt responded. "Well, yes, I'm an Israelite—from the tribe of Benjamin. Why do you ask?"

"I thought none of us were supposed to eat unclean meat, not just me."

"This is good meat, boy! It's less expensive than lamb, and everyone else eats it. Besides, those are old laws that don't apply to us anymore. We have bigger things to worry about than what we eat." Auntie walked away in a huff.

"I'm sorry," Samson said simply. He could tell he had hurt the woman's feelings, but he wasn't sure why. He didn't understand why one of his own people would purposely break the laws of God that were sent through Moses.

"It's all right, Samson," his father whispered to him. "Our people have mingled with the foreigners so long they have forgotten that we are God's chosen people. He has set us apart to be different from everyone else."

"Sometimes I don't like being different," Samson replied a bit sullenly.

Manoah absentmindedly stroked his son's long hair. "I know, but we are different because God doesn't want us to lose sight of what He has done for us and what He will do for us if we are faithful." He took a deep, shaky breath and pulled his son closer to him. He was quiet so long that Samson started to worry. "Oh, Samson, I think my brother is right," he finally continued. "I have been unfaithful by keeping you hidden away in the hills. Perhaps you should stay here and begin military training."

"Father, I don't understand. I thought I was learning how to be a shepherd."

"Samson, you remember the story your mother and I told you about the Lord appearing to us years ago?"

"Yes, I love that story."

"There's more that we haven't told you," Manoah continued cautiously. "The Lord told us that our Nazirite son would be set apart for a special work. You do know that *you* are that boy, right?"

Of course he knew he was the Nazirite child that the Lord had promised his parents. He had always known he was different, but he didn't know why. He nodded his head.

"The Lord has set you apart to free His people from the oppression of the Philistines. *You* are our deliverer!"

Samson took a deep breath and held it for a moment before letting it out slowly. He stared at his father with wide eyes, wondering if he had heard him right. "Me! A deliverer? How is that possible? What can I do against all the Philistines?"

"I don't know, son. Maybe you'll be a prophet like Deborah or a warrior like Gideon. I just don't know what God has planned for you yet. All I know is that you have to continue to stay faithful to your Nazirite vows and learn all you can from your cousin Joel."

"Why Joel? What is he supposed to teach me?"

"He was a soldier before he and his wife settled down in Mahaneh-dan. His father has told me many stories of his skill and bravery."

"Why isn't he a soldier anymore?" Samson asked as he peered across the fire at his rugged-looking cousin, sitting protectively next to his wife and baby daughter.

"He worked with a small band of rebel soldiers who traveled to various towns offering the people protection from the Philistines in exchange for food and shelter. They settled for a summer in Beersheba, and that is where he met his wife, Hannah. I believe she was a captive of the Philistines for a while before Joel met her, but none of us really knows her story."

"Do you know what caused those scars on her face?"

"No, but I have the feeling she has scars that run much deeper that we cannot see." Samson didn't quite understand, but he could tell Hannah was a sad, quiet woman. He looked across the fire at her again and wondered what the Philistines had done to her.

"Once Joel decided to marry Hannah, she begged him to take her away," Manoah continued. "Her parents had been killed, and the family she was staying with in Beersheba had no objections, so he brought her back here to his father's house and gave up fighting Philistines in order to keep her as far away from danger as possible."

"But the Philistines are so close to Mahaneh-dan. Don't they come here too?" Samson had spent his life watching for the large soldiers on horseback that rode through the hills occasionally, taking whatever they pleased. It just seemed to be an unavoidable danger that had to be lived with—like lions threatening the sheep.

"The Philistines are everywhere, but the men here in Mahaneh-dan are equipped to deal with them in their own way."

"How?" Samson asked as he picked at what food was left on his plate.

"The townspeople have established constant lookouts around the area. If the Philistines are seen coming this way, the lookouts will signal by blowing a horn. The women and children know to take as many of the animals as they can grab and hide out in the caves nearby until someone comes for them."

"Why do they have to hide? Why don't they just give the Philistines a tribute every year like we do?" Samson knew the routine at his house very well. Every year after the harvest, two armed soldiers would come banging on their door. As long as his parents cooperated and gave them a substantial portion of the crops as well as a few sheep, they were left in peace. Their small family lived alone on the side of the hill and had little to give, so the Philistines didn't waste much time on them.

"Having a large settlement has its advantages and disadvantages," Manoah answered. "Sometimes there is safety in numbers, but sometimes it just attracts more attention. As you know, Mahaneh-dan has a substantial flock of sheep, but they also have large vineyards just outside of town. They generate a lot of wealth from those grapes, and the Philistines want to make sure they get a portion of it. Unfortunately, they aren't satisfied with just the crops and animals. They've been known to take women and children as well."

"How can they do that? Why doesn't someone stand up to them?" Samson felt himself get angry, but he had no idea why.

"You probably don't remember Uncle Asahel's oldest son, Bilak. He died when you were very young. He tried to stand up to the Philistines when they threatened to take his wife and young son many years ago, and they killed him right here in the streets."

Samson hesitated as he tried to understand everything his father was telling him. "What happened to his wife and son?"

"That's them over there." Manoah pointed to a woman and boy about Samson's age who were sitting outside of the family circle. "You've probably never met them because they aren't involved in the family holidays. The only reason they're here now is that the boy tends the sheep, so it would be cruel not to let them eat with us."

"Why are they way over there? Why isn't anyone talking to them?"

"She's a Philistine. Bilak was a fool to marry her, but now that he's dead, it is my brother's responsibility to look after her and the boy. His name is Alvah, and I guess he's about your age—maybe a little older. Be careful around him and always remember he's half Philistine."

"Yes, but he's also half Israelite." Samson wasn't sure why he was defending the stranger.

"If he and his mother believed in the God of heaven, I would accept them with open arms; but they still worship Dagon like the other Philistines. It seems innocent enough, but it is a poison in our land that slowly causes us to turn away from God. I'm not saying you can't be kind to the boy; I just want you to be cautious."

"That's enough, you two," Uncle Asahel interrupted. "You've been over here whispering to each other all evening. Has your father decided to let you stay with us, Samson?"

The boy looked up at his father, waiting to see what his destiny would be.

"Yes," Manoah responded slowly, "I think he's ready."

CHAPTER 7

That night, Samson dozed by the fire, half listening to the conversations going on around him. At some point, he was carried into his uncle's house and placed on a sleeping mat in the middle of a crowded room. Though he was able to sleep through the adults celebrating, the blast from a distant horn caused him to spring awake immediately. The men scattered on the floor beside him were still groggy from too much wine and food, and most of them did not hear the warning blasts. But his father was beside him in a flash.

"Samson, get up. The Philistines are coming! Quickly, wake as many people as you can; then find the other children and follow them to safety."

Samson obeyed his father and began shaking the sleepy men next to him. He was surprised at how quickly the town came back to life. People were running around in the streets trying to hide armloads of valuables. His cousin's wife, Hannah, grabbed him by the arm and pulled him toward a crowd of children. She had her baby on her hip and a look of pure terror on her face.

"Alvah, let's go. Take us to the caves before the Philistines get here!" she shouted at the boy who was gathering the sheep.

Without a word, the strange half-Philistine boy took his shepherd's rod and started walking toward the edge of town. He seemed to know exactly where he was going, and the women and children in the group trusted him completely. It seemed odd to Samson that this boy who was so excluded from the family activities the night before was now responsible for leading them all to safety. But perhaps because he was a shepherd, he knew the best hiding places.

Samson didn't have much time to think about it; he just followed, like one of the sheep.

CHAPTER 7

The sky was starting to lighten in the east when the group reached a small stream cutting a path through the trees. Alvah lifted a young lamb onto his shoulders and started to climb the embankment on the north side of the stream. The terrain became slightly more rocky and steep, and Samson noticed his young cousin Deborah was struggling to maintain her footing. Without looking over his shoulder to see if anyone was watching, he took her hand and helped her climb. His small act of kindness made her face light up.

When Samson was sure they would both drop from exhaustion, Alvah announced that they were safe. He ushered the animals into a well-hidden cave and led the women and children in after them. Once inside, they were surrounded by complete darkness. Samson felt that familiar feeling of fear climb up his spine, so he silently prayed again to God for courage. He didn't feel any braver, but he did feel a little calmer. He noticed that the quiet whispers of the other children and their mothers slowly died off. Even the animals settled down and became quiet. Eventually, Samson nodded off. He woke not knowing where he was or how much time had passed. He decided to step outside the cave to see if he could tell what time it was.

When he stepped out of the cave, he had to blink several times in order for his eyes to adjust to the light. He felt as though he had been in the cave for days, but it looked like only a few hours had passed. His thoughts were interrupted by a voice nearby.

"Who are you?" It was the boy, Alvah, sitting on the ground under the branches of a broom tree that had just dropped the last of its yellow flowers.

"I'm Samson. I think we're cousins."

"Oh, you're Manoah's son. My name is Alvah, son of Bilak, grandson of your uncle Asahel. That probably does make us cousins or something."

Samson didn't tell the boy that he already knew all about him. Instead, he sat down next to him and studied the Philistine's appearance. He was surprised to find that Alvah didn't look any different from the other kids. In fact, he had the same dimple on his chin that Samson and his brothers had.

"You may not want to sit next to me," Alvah said bitterly. "I would hate to make you unclean or anything."

"You won't make me unclean, that is, unless you're dead," Samson said with a little snicker.

"I just know how picky you Jews are, and I imagine *you're* even worse with that vow you took."

Samson didn't know what to say, so he just sat silently next to his Philistine cousin. He absentmindedly picked up one of the yellow blossoms from the ground next to him and rubbed the soft petals between his fingers. "Alvah, why are we here? What's happening back in town?"

"One of the watchmen must have spotted Philistines coming to Mahaneh-dan. That's why you could hear horns off in the distance—that is their warning signal. The Philistines must have been waiting for the sheep-shearing celebration so they could come in while the men were all drunk and take all the wool."

"Oh no. My father's wool is there, and so are most of our animals. Will they take them?" Samson felt a sick knot tighten in his stomach.

"If I were you, I would worry more about your family than your precious animals and wool. Who knows what those soldiers will do to them."

Samson noticed a sad shadow cross Alvah's face. "They killed your father, didn't they?" he asked cautiously.

"Yes," Alvah replied simply. "He died to save me." His voice was almost a whisper.

Samson felt like crying at the thought of losing his father. What would happen to his mother and brothers? "We should go back and help the people in the town. We can't sit here hiding in a cave. We have to do something." Panic started to rise in Samson's throat.

"There's nothing we can do except stay here and wait for someone to get us. Besides, we have to watch the women and children."

Neither Alvah nor Samson had hair on their chins yet, but they were older and bigger than the other children in the cave. Since they both had experience as shepherds, they were the best "men" for the job. Samson silently agreed that they must stay and protect those who were weaker.

Just then a voice at the opening of the cave caused both boys to jump. It was a small girl rubbing the sleep out of her eyes. "Alvah, I'm hungry," she whimpered.

"I don't have any food, Deborah, but you can have some of this strong wine. Be careful not to drink too much of it though; it will make your head spin." He made a gesture to offer some to Samson, who refused even though his mouth was parched.

"Why do you drink that kind of juice?" Samson asked.

"Because I'm a shepherd," Alvah responded smugly.

"I'm a shepherd too, but I don't drink that."

Alvah snorted in disgust. "If I take new wine with me in the fields for days, it will go bad, especially when it's hot and sunny. This wine is fermented so it will last longer."

"Oh, well, I know something that is always fresh and never goes bad," Samson said, trying to sound older.

"What?"

"Water!" Samson responded.

"What is that, some kind of riddle or something?" Alvah asked. The little girl sitting between them scooted closer to Samson.

"I like riddles," she said. "Tell me another one."

Samson thought for a moment. "OK, here's one. What's worse than the Philistine soldiers and greater than God?"

"I don't know," Deborah answered, with a hint of a smile playing on her lips.

"Nothing!" Samson exclaimed triumphantly.

"That's a good one. You're smart," the little girl said as she cuddled closer to Samson. "I heard my father say that you're going to stay in Mahaneh-dan this summer so you can train to be a soldier like Uncle Joel."

"That is if there is a Mahaneh-dan left after the Philistines are finished with it," Alvah responded crossly.

Samson ignored Alvah's dark mood and tried his best to comfort the little girl whose bottom lip started to quiver at the thought of losing her home. "It'll be all right, Deborah. We're going to go back to Mahaneh-dan, and I'll learn to be a soldier so the Philistines won't be able to do this ever again."

She smiled adoringly up at Samson.

Alvah and Samson spotted movement in the distance, and they immediately jumped to their feet. Samson wished he had his sling and staff with him.

"You two get back in the cave," Alvah ordered.

Deborah obeyed, but Samson stayed where he was. "Do you have an extra sling?"

"No, find yourself some rocks and start throwing if you need to," Alvah replied.

Samson picked up a large rock for each hand and stood ready to attack at any sign of danger. He felt his pulse pounding in his ears, and his arms twitched with anticipation. They could see a man walking toward them, but they couldn't tell if he was friend or foe. The familiar sound of a horn put both the boys at ease.

"It's Uncle Asahel!" Samson exclaimed. "He's come to take us home."

The women and children in the cave began pouring out into the sunlight, rubbing their eyes as they emerged. In minutes, Uncle Asahel was fully recognizable, with a large smile spread across his dirty, tired face.

"Children, let's go home!" he called as Deborah ran into her grandfather's arms. "We are safe for the time being."

CHAPTER 8

The town Samson returned to was much different from the one he had left only a few hours earlier. Some of the houses had been burned. All of the storehouses had been emptied. The small family gardens looked as though they had been trampled by horses' hooves. The exhausted residents of Mahaneh-dan stood in small groups talking. Most of the men straightened their shoulders when they saw their wives and children returning. But some men were missing. That's when Samson saw a small group of men in the distance near a large acacia tree. He wandered over, hoping to find his father. As he got closer, he saw his father in the branches of the tree with a knife in his hand. He was cutting what looked like a long vine with something large hanging at the end. That's when Samson realized it was a man hanging from the branch. He gasped in horror when he noticed two more men lying on the ground under the tree with ropes around their necks.

"Father!" he yelled.

Manoah and the other men noticed Samson for the first time, and he was quickly ushered away from the scene, but he would never forget the horror of what he saw.

After a few minutes, his father came to him with fresh blood dripping down his bare arms and legs. Samson ran into his arms and cried freely. "Father, what happened to you? Did they hurt you?"

"No, son. No one hurt me. I'm bleeding from the thorns on the tree."

"What happened to those men?"

"Oh, Samson, I wish you hadn't seen that." He held his son close and stroked the back of his head. "Those men were killed by the Philistine soldiers. They did not want to surrender all of their wool, and they tried to fight. The soldiers burned their houses and hung their bodies as a lesson to all of us."

In the distance, Samson could hear the mourning cries of the families who just realized that their fathers and husbands had been killed.

"How can they do this?" Samson asked between sobs. "Why does God allow this to happen to His people?"

"I don't know, son. But I do know Yahweh has not abandoned us. He will show us a way out of this bondage. He will show *you* a way." He held his son out at arm's length and looked at his face as though it was the first time. "Someday, you will make our lives better. I know you will. Now, go help your cousin Alvah with the animals that were spared. I'm going to help prepare the men for burial. You must remember to stay away from the bodies. I don't want you breaking your Nazirite vow—especially now."

Samson did as his father asked and walked over to the animal enclosure where Alvah was trying to get the animals calmed down. That is when Samson realized that most of his father's herd had been taken. The only animals that remained were the ram and three ewes. He knew they had two doe goats back at home, but it was hardly enough to sustain their growing family. He worried again for his mother and brothers.

"Is all the wool gone?" he asked Alvah.

"Most of it. I think some of it was hidden away in the houses," he replied, as he checked the legs of one of Uncle Asahel's ewes.

"What are we going to do?"

"Don't worry, Samson. We still have the harvest in a few months. Enough food was hidden that we will survive until then."

"But my father's herd has been destroyed, and all the money he would have gotten for the wool is gone. How is he going to feed our family? I have two brothers at home, and my mother is going to have another baby the end of this year."

"I'm sure Uncle Asahel and the rest of your family will take care of you." Alvah sounded bitter as he continued his work. "Your people seem to be good at sticking together."

"They're your people, too, Alvah."

"Did you forget? I'm half Philistine. They'll hate me even more now. I might as well have set fire to the houses myself."

"They take care of you—and your mother. How can you be so ungrateful?"

"I should be grateful for being treated like a slave?" Alvah's face was red and his hands were shaking. He continued caring for the cut on the ewe's leg but ranted under his breath the entire time, as if Samson weren't even there. "One of these days, I'm going to run away and go to Timnah. My father should have just let them take me when I was little. Maybe the Philistines would treat me like family."

Just then, Joel's wife, Hannah, approached the animal enclosure. "Samson," she called out, completely ignoring Alvah, "I would like you and your father to join us for dinner. I'm sure you're very hungry. Please get cleaned up and come over to our place as soon as you are finished with what you are doing."

Alvah gave Samson a look that seemed to say, I told you so. "You'd better hurry; you don't want to keep *your* family waiting." Alvah's voice dripped with sarcasm.

Samson felt sad, but he didn't totally understand why. He hardly knew this boy, but he did think it was unfair that Alvah was being left out by the family. Was it really so bad that he was half Philistine? After all, it wasn't his fault. Samson hesitantly followed Hannah to her house, but he looked over his shoulder occasionally to watch the lonely Alvah and the animals.

CHAPTER 9

Joel and Hannah lived in one of the rooms attached to the back of Uncle Asahel's home. In Mahaneh-dan, it was easy to tell what the size of a family was just by looking at the house. Most homes started as a small one-room dwelling, but as the family grew, so did the house. Attachments were added on as sons grew up and took wives. Uncle Asahel's home had three apartments added to the main living area—one for each of his two surviving sons and one for the widow and child of his oldest son who had been killed by the Philistines. Most of the meals were eaten together in the common courtyard, but Joel's wife, Hannah, was a very private woman, so she had a small cooking area set up behind their apartment so she could be alone with her family when the crowd became too much for her.

Hannah led Samson to a basin of water and instructed him to wash while she finished the meal preparations. Joel rose from where he was seated by the fire.

"Hello, Samson. I'm glad you could join us. Your father should be along soon. Come sit with me."

Samson quickly washed then found a place next to his older cousin.

"I understand you will be staying here in Mahaneh-dan this summer."

Samson nodded shyly in response.

"Hannah and I have been talking, and we think it would be best if you stay with us. You'll still be very close to your uncle, but this will give me an opportunity to spend more time with you. I have a lot to teach you in a short time." Joel rose from his seat and rummaged through a pile of rags near the house. "I got this for you. I thought it would be helpful for your training."

40

Joel handed Samson a heavy iron sword. The boy almost dropped it but recovered quickly.

"Where did you get it?" Samson asked in awe as he fingered the rough carving on the handle.

"I took it from a soldier I killed this morning."

"You killed a Philistine soldier today?" Samson exclaimed.

"*Sssh,* don't let Hannah hear you. It will frighten her. She'll worry about their coming back for revenge."

Samson thought for a moment as he examined the sword. "They *will* come back for revenge, won't they?" he asked quietly.

"Yes," Joel answered simply. "That is why your training must start now. I don't know how much time I will have with you."

"What will they do to you?"

"I'm not sure if anyone saw me kill the man; there was so much confusion. The other Philistines may not even know he's missing until they get back to Timnah. But I'm sure they will come back to find out what happened to him, and they won't stop until they find out who's responsible. I plan to turn myself in before they do any more damage to the rest of the family. Perhaps they will just take me and leave everyone else alone."

Samson was about to respond, but Joel held his finger to his lips when he saw Hannah emerge from the apartment. Samson quickly tucked the sword under the blanket he was sitting on.

"Where is your father, Samson? I thought he would be here by now." A look of concern crossed her face. "You don't think something happened to him do you, Joel?"

"No, dear, he will be here soon. He was helping with a cleanup project outside of town. I'm sure he would want us to start without him."

"Very well then; let's eat now before the baby wakes up. She'll probably start crying as soon as I take my first bite of food." Samson could tell by her face that she wouldn't mind at all if the baby interrupted her meal.

Joel said a blessing over the food, and Hannah served them steaming bowls of lentil stew and pieces of thick, dark bread.

"I think we will have enough food to last until the harvest, though we won't have meat to eat again for quite a while," she said as she ladled a bowl of stew for herself.

Samson was surprised to see Hannah so relaxed and open. He had never heard her speak at a family meal before. He felt more at ease with her now. It was almost as comfortable as being with his mother. Perhaps it wouldn't be so bad staying with them for the summer. The thought of it made him want to pick up the hidden sword again.

As the three ate and talked casually, Manoah approached the fire. He washed the dirt and blood from his face and arms and joined the trio without saying a word. Hannah immediately rose to serve him. An obvious tension now hung over them as they finished their meal in silence.

"I will return home tomorrow to make sure your mother and brothers are safe," Manoah finally said as he set his half-eaten dinner aside. "You will stay here with Joel and Hannah and begin training immediately. I'm going to my brother's house to sleep. I'll see you all in the morning." He rose to leave. "Thank you for dinner, Hannah. I'm sorry I wasn't better company."

Samson watched as his father rounded the corner to go to Uncle Asahel's room. He had never seen his father look so grim before. He wished he could ease his father's worry and lighten his load. Maybe someday he could.

CHAPTER 10

The next morning the family watched as Manoah departed with what was left of his belongings. Samson bit down on his lower lip to keep from crying. Joel and Hannah stood close by. As soon as Manoah was out of sight, Joel put his hand on Samson's shoulder and whispered, "It's time to start."

The former soldier led his new apprentice out of the village. The two reached a large pasture area where they could see sheep grazing in the distance. Samson thought he could make out the figure of his Philistine cousin, Alvah, watching over the herd.

"Get your sword, Samson," Joel instructed as he handed a large sack to him.

Samson grunted under the weight of the bag as he set it on the ground with a thud. He felt the cold handle of the sword and pulled it free from the other iron weapons in the bag. Before Samson knew what was happening, Joel had pulled a hidden sword from under his cloak and was charging toward him. Samson tried to defend himself, but Joel was on him too fast, knocking him onto his backside. He gasped for air as Joel lifted him back onto his feet.

"Be alert, Samson. You must always be ready for attack." He backed away from the boy as he talked. "Now, let's try it again." Joel raised his sword and charged again.

Samson planted his feet and held his heavy sword out to block the charge, but the unfamiliar weight of the iron knocked him off balance, sending him sprawling to the ground.

"How am I supposed to do anything with this thing? This sword is as big as I am," Samson whined as he picked himself up off the ground again.

"The Philistines fight with iron, so you must learn to fight back," Joel replied as he readied himself to charge a third time.

Samson braced himself for another blow, trying hard not to cry. *God, help me,* he silently prayed as he watched Joel charge with his sword lifted above his head. At that moment, something changed. Samson could hear his pulse pounding in his ears as he watched Joel moving toward him in slow motion. He could see the dust fly up from the ground as Joel's feet touched down. He lifted the iron blade in front of his face as if it weighed no more than his slender shepherd staff. His eyes narrowed, and his breath filled his lungs as Joel moved closer. He watched his own arm and hand move as though they belonged to someone else. His sword rose just as Joel's came down and met it with a ringing clang that vibrated in Samson's ears. His right elbow moved back ever so slightly, and with a force that was completely foreign to the boy, he pushed both his sword and his cousin's with such power that Joel had to take several steps backward to keep from falling.

Joel quickly recovered only to find the boy charging toward him with the heavy sword raised above his head. At first, Joel was afraid of injuring the boy, so his moves were strictly defensive, but it didn't take long for the soldier to realize it wasn't the child who was in danger of getting hurt.

"Samson!" he shouted as he used his height advantage to escape the boy's reach. "Samson, stop!"

Samson lowered his sword and stared at his cousin with a look of shock and confusion written on his face. "What was that?" Joel stammered as he sheathed his sword.

"Oh, I'm sorry," Samson stammered as he shook his head. "I don't know what happened."

Joel laughed out loud and plopped down in the dirt. Samson just stood frozen in place, staring at the hand that still gripped the dead Philistine's sword.

"Maybe we'll practice with wooden swords for a while," Joel said once he caught his breath. "You're strong enough to really hurt someone with a piece of iron in your hand."

Samson lay down the blade and sank into the dirt, feeling like his legs were made of soft clay. That's when he saw Alvah standing off in the distance, watching the entire scene. Joel followed his gaze and called out to the boy. "Alvah, did you see that? Our cousin Samson is a warrior! Those Philistines had better watch themselves. This boy will be our deliverer!"

Alvah didn't respond. Instead, he turned and ran back to his flock of sheep.

CHAPTER 11

Samson spent the next several weeks by Joel's side, learning everything he could. Joel taught him how to use a bow and arrow and how to consistently hit his target with a sling and stone. When the lessons on hand-to-hand combat began, Alvah was recruited to be a sparring partner for Samson. Even though Samson's strength was obvious, Joel was much too big for the fight to be fair. Joel made the arrangements for someone else to watch the sheep, and he took the two boys to a soft grassy area to begin the next lesson.

Alvah had been watching as much of the training as he could from his perch on the hillside overlooking the flock. He had seen Samson's strength and skill, but he didn't hesitate to take an opportunity to show off his own talents. The years alone in the wilderness had given Alvah plenty of opportunities to fight predators. This practice, combined with the anger that burned inside his heart, made him a force to be reckoned with. He hoped that if he could beat Samson, maybe his family would see him as something more than just a shepherd. He silently prayed to his god, Dagon, that he would be victorious. To him, this was not a sparring match; this was a war.

Joel instructed the boys on the best ways to attack an enemy. He showed them both how to move forward and throw the opponent off balance. He then taught them defensive moves that would protect the face and head if the enemy was getting the upper hand. Both boys absorbed every word and were eager to try the new techniques. As soon as Joel backed away, Alvah charged at his younger cousin immediately, throwing him to the ground. Samson couldn't hide his fear when he saw the anger and hatred in Alvah's eyes. Joel was there in a flash to pull Alvah off of Samson.

"What are you trying to do, Alvah? Take it easy. He's just a child!" Joel reprimanded, as he pulled the still swinging Alvah away from his cousin.

Once Alvah was calm again, Joel told them to continue. This time Alvah approached his opponent more slowly and cautiously. He had to keep his head if he was going to defeat his enemy. Samson watched every move Alvah made, waiting for an opportunity to strike. Around and around both boys moved, looking for an opening. Alvah lunged, but Samson moved away just in time.

"Come here, you long-haired baby," he growled as he reached out again to try to grab Samson. "I'll show you who's the warrior in this family."

Samson didn't completely understand where Alvah's anger was coming from. Again Alvah lunged and Samson ducked.

"Some hero you are," Alvah hissed. "You're not so brave when you have a real opponent, are you? Joel has been going easy on you, but I won't." Alvah finally got a hold of Samson's arm and pulled him closer. Samson twisted away and regained his footing.

"Take it easy, Alvah. We're just practicing," Samson panted.

"Where is your god now, Samson?" Alvah lunged and missed. "You're weak and your god is weak. He's been ignoring his people for years, and now he has forgotten you too."

Samson breathed deeply and felt his heart quicken in his chest. "Don't talk about my God that way, Alvah," he warned, as he wove away from Alvah's long reach.

Alvah saw that his insult had hit its mark, and he laughed to himself as he threw a punch toward Samson's face. His fist did not fly as true as his words and connected with nothing but air. In the brief moment that he was off balance, Samson saw an opening, and he flew at Alvah with all of his strength. He felt the blood pumping through his veins, moving to feed the muscles in his arms and legs. He saw the flash of fear in Alvah's eyes and the sweat beading on his lip. Samson leapt upward grabbing hold of Alvah around the waist. Using the momentum behind him, he threw the bigger boy down on the ground and straddled him while his arms and fists flew wildly at Alvah's face. Joel quickly pulled Samson away.

"Stop, Samson. He's down! You've beaten him," Joel commanded, as he shook Samson back into reality.

Alvah stayed on the ground but rolled over onto his stomach to let the blood from his nose run into the grass. Dagon had failed him again. He felt Samson tap him on the shoulder. When he rolled over, he saw his cousin's hand extended to help him up. Alvah slapped it away and rose on his own.

"I don't need you, Samson," he hissed as he slowly walked away. "I don't need any of you."

CHAPTER 12

Alvah did not return home that night or the next day. Only his mother and Samson seemed to notice his disappearance, but even they were not given much time to worry about where he could have gone. By early evening, a new crisis arose. The familiar sound of a distant horn sent the town scrambling to their designated hiding places. Before Hannah, her baby, and Samson could run off with the others, Joel grabbed them and pulled them into the house.

"Samson, you take Hannah and the baby to your father's house in Zorah. Stay off the main road, and watch for Philistines traveling back to Timnah. Do you understand me?"

"But what about my training?" Samson asked.

"I've taught you everything I can. Get your sword, Samson, and leave. Now!"

Hannah clung to her husband and cried. "No, Joel, you come with us."

"I've been hiding long enough. I have to face them now, or they will never leave us alone. I killed a soldier, and they will want revenge. I can't let them take it out on the entire town."

"They'll kill you, or worse, take you as a slave. You don't know what they do to prisoners . . ." Her voice trailed off again as she sobbed.

"You'll be safe with Samson. God has His hand on this boy. He will protect you." Joel turned his attention to Samson. "Remember, stay off the main road and out of sight. Don't let the Philistines see you no matter what. I'm giving you my family to protect. I know you won't let me down. Now, get them out of here before it's too late."

Samson ran outside and grabbed the bundle that contained his hidden sword. He then took Hannah's hand and led her and the crying baby from the house.

"God go with you!" Joel called as they left. He then marched deliberately to the center of town to face the coming Philistines.

Eventually, Hannah stopped fighting and followed Samson willingly. Deep down, she knew she would only endanger herself and her child if she went back. The baby slept fitfully in the makeshift sling she had fastened over her shoulder as they moved on in silence.

Occasionally Samson would stop to make sure they weren't being followed. His keen eyes scanned the horizon for billowing dust from Philistine horses. Samson knew the way back to his father's house, but avoiding the road made the trip much more difficult. Hannah never complained, but at one point she dropped next to a terebinth tree to rest.

"We have to keep going," Samson said. "My father's house is not far. You can rest there."

"How can I rest anywhere?" she whispered.

Samson sat next to her and protectively placed his small hand on her back. "My parents and I will take care of you. You'll be safe with us."

"Yes, but what about Joel? I know what those monsters will do to him when they get their hands on him . . ." Her voice broke and she began to cry quietly.

"They hurt you, didn't they?" Samson asked cautiously.

All she could do was nod as the tears streamed down her scarred cheeks.

"I won't let them hurt you again," Samson said, sounding more like a man than a boy. "Come on. We're almost there." He rose and held his hand out to her. She reluctantly took it and stood next to him, adjusting the sleeping baby in her sling.

"You're very brave for a child," she said softly as they walked on. "I'm glad you don't know what fear is yet, but I'm afraid someday you will."

"I've been afraid before, but I knew God was with me, and it helped me to be brave."

"You and Joel have so much faith in this invisible God. How do you know He's there? How can He protect you if you can't see Him or talk to Him?"

"He's there," Samson replied simply. "I see Him and talk to Him all the time."

Hannah just watched the boy curiously and continued to follow.

After a few more minutes of walking, Samson spotted movement on the road coming from the north. "Quick, hide!" he exclaimed as he pulled Hannah behind a large rock. "I think it's Philistine soldiers re-turning from Mahaneh-dan." Samson watched until the group was closer. Sure enough, it was five Philistine soldiers on horseback with a bound man half running, half dragging behind them. There was also a woman and a boy walking with them, but they were not tied up like prisoners. Samson gasped when he finally realized who it was. "They have Joel," he whispered. "He's not dead, and he doesn't look like he's hurt."

Hannah started to get up from behind her hiding place, but Samson pushed her back down. "There's someone else with them, but I can't quite—oh, no." He broke off in shock.

"What is it, Samson?"

"It's Alvah and his mother, but they don't look like they are being taken against their will."

Just then, Hannah's baby started to fuss. Hanna held her close and tried to comfort her, but the cries became louder.

Samson watched as the Philistines continued to move on toward Timnah, apparently unable to hear the baby over the sound of their horses' hooves, but then he saw Alvah hesitate and look around. Samson held his breath as he watched Alvah say something to his mother and then slowly walk toward them.

"Hannah, run. Take the baby and run up the hillside. The horses won't be able to follow you up there. Just take cover and hide until I get there."

She tried to object, but when she saw the figure moving toward them, she quickly obeyed and ran from rock to rock until she was safely up the hill.

"There's no point hiding; I know you're there," Alvah called when he was only paces away from the rock Samson still crouched behind.

Samson stood up and walked forward to meet his cousin, feeling a strange mixture of relief and dread. It looked as though the Philistine soldiers had continued on their way, but there was no telling what Alvah was capable of, even on his own.

"Are you alone?" Alvah asked as he scanned the area behind Samson.

"I don't see anyone else here, do you?"

"No, I guess not. You probably just ran off on your own when things got bad back in Mahaneh-dan. Are you running back to Mommy and Daddy now that Joel isn't around to protect you?"

Samson didn't answer, but he could feel his pulse speed up and his fists clench.

Alvah must have seen a warning flash in Samson's eyes, because he kept his distance. His nose and upper lip were still swollen from the sparring match. As brave as Alvah may have acted, he wasn't prepared to go fist to fist with his young cousin again.

"What are you doing with those soldiers, Alvah?"

"I'm with them now. When I left Mahaneh-dan, I went to Timnah to find my mother's family. The soldiers there were very nice to me, especially after I told them what Joel did to their missing friend."

"You turned Joel in? How could you do that? He's your family."

"Those Israelites don't treat me like family! I'm a Philistine—and they never let me forget it. I'm going back to my people and back to my god, Dagon. I'm tired of hiding and trying to fit in where I don't belong. The soldiers have promised to protect my mother and me in exchange for Joel. I think it's a pretty good deal."

Samson didn't know what to say. His father was right when he had warned Samson to be cautious of this boy.

"Don't worry, Samson, no one else in Mahaneh-dan was hurt; they wanted only Joel."

"What will they do to him?"

"I don't know. Maybe they'll sell him off as a slave, or maybe they'll use him for sparring practice." Alvah laughed bitterly. "Either way, you'll never see him again. So much for your great warrior training. You can just go off to your father's house and hide away in the hills with your sheep."

"And what about you, Alvah? Do you really think the Philistines will keep their promise to you? What makes you think you can trust them?"

"Don't you worry about me. I can take care of myself."

"But Alvah, your family—"

"I don't want anything to do with you and your family!" Alvah spat.

There didn't seem to be anything else to say. Samson slowly turned and walked away, somehow knowing that Alvah didn't have the strength or courage to make him stay.

CHAPTER 13

Samson caught up with Hannah and cautiously led her and the baby the rest of the way to his parents' house. As the sun continued to sink into the western horizon, Samson quickened his pace. He knew what kind of predators lurked in the wilderness after dark, and he wasn't eager to face any of them.

In the distance, Samson could see his home on the hillside. His mother had already lit the lamp for the evening, and the warm glow coming from the lone window pulled him in like a moth. He grabbed Hannah's hand, and the two ran the rest of the way.

When they reached the house, Samson pushed the door open and ran in with Hannah shyly following behind him. They found Manoah sitting at the table with a candle and a scroll spread out before him. Samson's two brothers were sprawled out on the floor listening to their father read. Sarai sat nearby mending a cloak that rested on her growing belly. Everyone stopped what they were doing and turned in shock when Samson burst into the room. His mother leapt to her feet and embraced her oldest son. Samson clung to her with unexplainable tears streaming down his face. Manoah rose more slowly and went to the door to close it securely.

"Why are you here, son?" he asked, his concern obvious. "Why is Hannah with you? Where is Joel?"

"*Shhh,* Manoah. Let them wash the dust off of their feet before you start interrogating them," Sarai said as she led Hannah to a stool and helped her untie the sleeping baby from the sling. The two women then quickly and efficiently changed the soiled clothes wrapped around the little girl and placed her in the cradle that stood nearby waiting for the newest baby to arrive. Sarai then washed her guest's feet and offered her a drink. Samson helped himself to a large drink of water as he splashed his face and hands clean.

"There now," Manoah said as everyone was finally seated. "Tell us what is happening."

Hannah sat silently with her eyes downcast as Samson explained Alvah's betrayal and Joel's capture.

"What is that?" Manoah asked, motioning toward the door where Samson had dropped his belongings when he came barging in.

Samson pulled the large iron sword from the bundle and showed it to his father. "This is the weapon Joel took from the Philistine he killed. He gave it to me."

"We must hide this," Manoah replied, looking concerned. "If the soldiers come here and find this, who knows what they will do to us."

"Joel taught me how to use it."

"That's fine, but you are still just a boy. For now, we will put it away for safekeeping." Manoah took the sword, wrapped it in cloth, and placed it in a covered hole in the hard dirt floor where he kept the family valuables.

"Father, what will we do about Joel?"

"I don't know if we can do anything," Manoah replied.

"But we know the soldiers are taking him to Timnah. We have to try to rescue him."

Manoah chuckled without humor. "What are an old man and a little boy going to do against an army of Philistines?"

"Maybe we can get someone to help."

"No, Samson. We don't want to bring trouble down on our heads. We've seen what those soldiers do to anyone who tries to stand up to them. Joel is a strong man. He will be able to take care of himself."

"But, we can't just leave him there—"

"Enough!" Manoah snapped, sounding sterner than he intended. "We are not going to put ourselves or the rest of our family in danger." He turned to Hannah and softened his voice. "You will stay here with us. We will make sure you and the baby are taken care of."

Hannah did not look up or reply, but Samson was sure he saw her tears hit the floor near her feet.

CHAPTER 14

Before dawn the next morning, the family was awakened by a soft tap on the door. Samson rubbed the sleep out of his eyes and walked into the main living area of the house where his parents were already warmly greeting a man dressed in a dark cloak.

"Who's here?" he asked sleepily.

The strange man turned toward him and removed the hood that had been covering his head and face.

"What, don't you recognize your uncle Asahel?" He smiled at the boy, but he did not look happy.

"Why are you here? What's happening?" Samson asked. Both of his parents gave him that look that said he was talking when he should have been listening, so he quickly sat down out of the way. Hannah was already up nursing her baby in a private corner of the house, listening to everything that was going on.

"There are more men coming." Asahel spoke quickly to his brother. "I've instructed them to travel either alone or in small groups so they don't attract any attention. I traveled under the cover of darkness so I could get here without being seen. We will go to Timnah tonight and get Joel."

"We're going to rescue Joel?" Samson jumped to his feet.

"Samson!" both of his parents scolded, and he quietly sat back down.

"What do you have in the way of weapons, Manoah?" Uncle Asahel continued as though Samson had not even spoken.

"I have nothing but a sling and a small dagger, but they won't be any use against an army. How can you possibly think we can get Joel out of Timnah without being killed? Even if we do get him, you know the Philistines will return and burn every house in their path until they find him."

"He's my son!" Asahel barked. "I will not leave him there! You don't have to help me, but I will at least try to save him."

"I'll help you, Uncle!" Samson interjected again.

Asahel looked at the boy with so much love and gratitude in his eyes that Samson thought he might cry.

"You will not!" Manoah exclaimed.

"At least someone in this house has faith," Asahel said as he glared at his younger brother. "The Lord Himself came to you, Manoah, and still you doubt Him! What is the matter with you? If God is with your boy, which I believe He is, then why would you hesitate to let him help rescue his cousin?"

"Because he could be killed!" Manoah snapped back. "It's my duty to protect him until he's old enough . . ." His voice broke and he could not finish.

Asahel softened and put his hand on his brother's shoulder. "I know you're afraid; I am too. Remember, I watched as they killed my oldest son, and I did nothing. I cannot stand by and watch them take my youngest away from me now."

Hannah rose from her corner and stood to her full height. "I will go with you, Father. I will help you rescue Joel too."

"But, Hannah, you know what they could do to you," Manoah said.

"No one knows better than I do," she said softly. "I was their slave for two years before I was released by the sympathetic wife of my owner. I watched the Philistine soldiers kill my parents, and during the two years I was their prisoner, I wished they had killed me too. I've been afraid ever since I was a girl, but I'm tired of being afraid." She turned to Samson. "Joel said God is with this boy, and I believe him. If Samson goes with us, maybe God will help us get Joel back. We can't be afraid forever."

"A woman, a boy, and two old men are going to march into Timnah and take a prisoner. It's impossible!" Manoah mumbled.

"Father, you've always told me nothing is too big for God. Did you mean only for Noah or Joseph or Moses? What about us? Don't you think God can help us like He helped them?"

Sarai put her hand softly on her husband's shoulder. "You know he's right, Manoah. Have faith."

"Very well." Manoah sighed. "But we will not spend the day gathering weapons. We will spend the day praying for God's help and guidance."

CHAPTER 15

Throughout the day, men from Mahaneh-dan trickled into Samson's home. The first to arrive was Joel's older brother, Caleb, who came with two others whom Samson recognized as Uncle Asahel's neighbors. By the early evening, Samson counted twelve men—including himself. The last to arrive was a small, hunched-over farmer with weak eyes. When he announced that no one else was able to come, Samson felt his heart sink a bit. He had to admit that the group did not look like enough to overtake the Philistines, but he continued to pray while the adults discussed the plan.

"I will take Samson and Manoah into town first to check things out," Asahel explained. "I don't think the three of us will draw much attention."

"I want to go with you," Hannah said softly from her place in the corner. "If you are traveling with a woman and child, we will look like only a family going to town to trade goods."

"Very well, Hannah, you will come too," Asahel continued. "After the sun sets, the rest of you will meet us by the eastern gates of the city, and we will decide on the best course of action from there."

The group prayed together one last time; then Samson left with his father, uncle, Hannah, and the baby. They carried baskets of produce so it appeared that they were going to trade in the market. It didn't take them long to reach Timnah, and when they did, they walked easily past the guards at the gate. Samson was shocked by the number of people gathered inside the city. He couldn't help but feel overwhelmed. Timnah was a busy seaside town ruled by Philistines. The center of town contained booths where vendors sold fruits, vegetables, wine, fish, and many other goods from faraway lands. Samson had never been to such a large town before. Even though Timnah was close to their home, Samson's father always avoided the Philistine town and went to the Israelite city of Eshtaol to do his trading.

Once inside the market area, the group separated as Asahel and Hannah strolled through the booths trying to trade goods and gather information. Samson and his father continued west toward the large expanse of blue sea. The smell of salt and the noise of the market filled Samson's senses.

"Samson, you sit here for a few minutes and rest. I'm going to talk to those men to see if they know anything about Joel." Manoah left his son and walked over to where a group of fishermen and a merchant were standing nearby, haggling over the price of their catch.

Samson watched his father for a while, but he was soon distracted by all the other action going on around him. Three soldiers slowly walked past Samson as if he were completely invisible. They laughed and talked while the boy studied them. Of course he had seen Philistine soldiers several times before, but this was the first time he had the opportunity to really look at them. They were huge men, much taller than his father and uncle. On their heads, they wore helmets topped with red feathers that were held in place by leather chinstraps. The partial armor they wore over their chests and backs resembled the scales of a fish, probably to honor their fish-god, Dagon. All three were armed with a large straight sword like the one he had hidden in the floor of his father's house. Samson wondered where they were going. Maybe they knew where Joel was. Without thinking, he rose to his feet and casually walked behind them. The soldiers strolled past the pier where the fishermen gathered. They continued toward a cluster of buildings and stopped for a moment to talk to a group of women standing around in the street. Samson couldn't help but stare. They were so different from the women he was used to seeing. Their heads were completely uncovered, revealing long, flowing hair. Their lips and eyes seemed to be painted, making them look larger and fuller than those of the women he was used to. He found them so strange, but somehow beautiful. The soldiers walked on, and Samson followed at a safe distance.

After several twists and turns down narrow streets, Samson was completely lost. For the first time since he had left his father, he realized he might not be able to find his way back. He started to panic, but when he realized that the soldiers had stopped walking, he quickly hid next to a building. It looked as though the soldiers had reached their post. All three of the men walked inside a small wooden building, and three other soldiers came out. Samson snuck closer to the building to see if he could tell what was inside. Through the window he could hear the men talking, but he couldn't make out what they were saying. He saw a large platform behind the building that looked like some sort of stage. On the far side of the platform he could barely make out something on the ground that glistened in the sunlight. He crept toward the light and realized it was iron bars covering a long, shallow trench. All of a sudden, he felt something reach up through the bars and grab his ankle. He almost screamed, but quickly contained himself. He easily shook his foot free and jumped away from the bars.

"Who's down there?" he whispered in a shaky voice.

He heard a man's voice, but he was speaking a strange language that Samson didn't understand. He lay down on his stomach so he could see inside. The light from the sun shone down into the pit, and he could see several men and a woman with a small child sitting in the dirt under the iron bars.

"Why are you down there? Is this some kind of prison?" he whispered down into the ditch.

"We've been taken from our homes," a woman's voice responded. She had a slight accent, but Samson had no trouble understanding what she was saying. "We're going to be sold as slaves in the market tomorrow. Can you help us?"

"I'm just a child . . ." he started to say but he was interrupted as a man scrambled over from a far corner of the darkness.

"Samson, is that you?" It was Joel! He reached his hand through the bars and Samson took hold of it.

"Yes, it's me. We've come to save you."

Just then a Philistine soldier moved toward him, shouting.

"Don't worry about anything, Joel. We'll come back for you tonight," Samson whispered, just before he rose to his feet and ran.

He started to make his way back toward the sea, knowing that it was in the same direction as the setting sun, but then he remembered the group's plan to meet at the eastern gate of the town after sunset. He turned and quickly started walking east through the maze of streets. With every step he took, he silently prayed that God would help him find his way back to his father and that they would somehow be able to get Joel out of that pit.

CHAPTER 16

After hours of walking, Samson's legs felt weak, and his stomach growled with hunger. It was getting dark, and he was afraid he wouldn't find his way out of the city on time to meet his family. He saw a crowd gathered outside of a large white building, and he walked toward them, hoping someone there could direct him toward the eastern gate. Before he realized what was happening, he was engulfed by the crowd of people.

He fought against the pull of the bodies moving him into the building, but he couldn't break free. He couldn't see much, but he guessed the crowd had moved him into some type of temple. The floor beneath his feet was made of cold stone, and the smell of smoke and incense filled his nose. Once inside, the crowd thinned out enough that Samson could move a little more freely. He found himself in a large open room that reminded him of a cave carved out of white stone. Torches along the walls provided light, but the atmosphere was dark and gloomy. In the center of the room, he saw a huge statue carved out of the same white stone that the building was made of. Several people lay face down on the floor in front of the statue. Samson's curiosity moved him closer so he could see what it was. He stood looking up at the huge carved figure of a crowned man who, instead of legs, had a tail like a fish. Time seemed to stand still as he stood with his mouth open and his feet frozen in place until he felt a hand on his shoulder, causing him to jump with fright.

"You must be lost." Samson looked into the eyes of a strange woman with a painted face and kind eyes. "Are you a Hebrew?" she asked, gently leading the boy away from the statue. "You're going to get yourself in trouble standing in front of Dagon like that. Don't you know he's a god, and he should be worshiped?"

"That's Dagon?" Samson stuttered in response.

"Of course." The woman replied warmly.

"But it's just a stature," Samson said innocently.

"You *must* be a Hebrew. Come on; you don't belong in here."

She guided Samson toward the door. "It's obvious you did not intend to come into Dagon's temple. Where are you trying to go?"

"I'm trying to get back to my father. We're supposed to meet outside of the eastern gate. I'm sure he's very worried about me." Samson choked back tears.

"Now, now, don't cry, little man. I'll help you find your way. Come on."

Samson followed, sniffing back the unwanted tears. "Why are you being nice to me? I thought all the Philistines hated Israelites."

The woman chuckled softly. "You'd be surprised how many Israelites come here to worship. Dagon will accept sacrifices and offerings from anyone."

"But I'm not here to sacrifice to Dagon. I believe in the God of heaven," Samson replied standing taller than he had before.

"Well between you and me, I don't really care who you worship. I work in the temple only because it pays the bills. I have a daughter almost your age, and she needs to eat." She stopped walking and pointed to the familiar gate in the distance. "There's the eastern gate, but I don't think it's a good idea for you to go right past the guards. A child traveling alone might attract attention. Besides, they'll be locking the gates soon, but don't worry; this city isn't very well fortified. There are openings all along this side of town where you can pass back and forth unnoticed. Take this street here, and it will lead you right out of town. You can get back in this way, too, if you ever want to come back to visit me." She leaned over and gave him a kiss on the cheek. Samson could smell the fragrant oils that she had rubbed on her skin and hair. "You're sweet," she said as she turned and walked away. "Now, be careful. I hope your god protects you, little man."

Samson watched her walk away. He had never seen anyone so beautiful in his life. Part of him wanted to run after her and follow her back to Dagon's temple, but then he remembered his family. He had to get back to his father and rescue Joel. He followed the directions the woman had given him and quickly made his way out of Timnah.

The sky continued to darken, and Samson was afraid he would be left alone all night. Just when that familiar feeling of panic started to rise up in his chest, he heard his father call to him.

"Samson, is that you?" A dark figure walked toward him cautiously.

"Father, it's me." He ran into his father's arms and held on tightly. Manoah led his son to the group from Mahaneh-dan, who were standing off in the distance hidden by the shadows of a large tree.

"Asahel, I found him," Manoah called as he reached the group. Even in the dark, Samson could see they were all relieved. Several men patted him on the back, and his uncle kissed him on both cheeks.

"I've found Joel," Samson exclaimed when the greetings were finished. "He is in a ditch covered with iron bars on the western side of town. There are three guards in a building near the ditch, but none of them were watching the prisoners too closely. I think we can sneak in there and get him out, but we have to do it tonight. He will be sold in the market tomorrow."

"How will we get the bars open, Samson? Was there some kind of lock?" Manoah asked.

"Yes, but I think the guards had the keys inside."

"Can you take us to him?" Uncle Asahel asked Samson.

"Yes. I even know a way to get back into the city without having to go past the guards."

"Excellent. Manoah and I will follow the boy so we can get a better idea of what we're working with. The rest of you stay here and look after Hannah and the baby. We'll be back soon." Uncle Asahel put his hand on Samson's shoulder. "Let's go."

CHAPTER 17

Samson wove his way through the streets and back past the temple of Dagon, where he hesitated for only a moment, hoping to catch a glimpse of his new friend. The market was closed, but the streets were still filled with people. Samson wondered why they weren't home with their families.

It didn't take long for Samson to find the place where Joel was being held. He pointed out the guard building to his father and uncle, and the three quietly crept past the windows and made their way to the ditch.

"Joel, are you there?" Uncle Asahel whispered.

"Yes, Father. I'm here. There are others here too. We must get them out."

Asahel and Manoah both examined the bars and the large lock that held them in place.

"I don't know how we're going to get this opened, son, but we'll come up with something," Asahel answered.

"Without a key, we'll never get it open," Manoah whispered to his older brother.

Samson lay down on the ground and tried to dig a hole next to the bars. If he had a week, he may have been able to make an opening big enough for himself but not for Joel. He started to lose hope. *God, what are we going to do?* he silently prayed. He looked down into the ditch and saw a woman sitting with a young child on her lap. An old man sat in another corner praying a familiar Hebrew prayer. That's when Samson heard a voice that sounded as though it was carried on the wind. *"Pull,"* the Voice whispered. Samson looked around, trying to figure out who had spoken to him. His father and uncle were still talking softly to each other. The people in the ditch were silent except for the hoarse prayers of the old man.

CHAPTER 17

"Pull." The Voice came again, more urgent this time. Without a second thought, Samson began to pull on the bars. Nothing happened, but he continued to pull with all his strength. Joel saw his efforts, and he rose to help.

"Samson, these bars are made of iron; we can't bend them," Joel whispered.

"Just pull!" Samson grunted.

"The soldiers are going to hear us. We have to go!" Manoah whispered, frantically trying to lift his son off the ground. "Samson, we have to go now! We'll come back later once we have a plan and more men to help us."

Samson didn't hear the soldiers scrambling around in the shack. He didn't hear his father urging him to leave. All he heard was the small Voice telling him *"Pull,"* so he did.

"Samson, leave. If the soldiers get you, you'll be no help to me," Joel called from inside the hole.

"Manoah, come! We have to leave him!" Asahel grabbed hold of his brother and tore him away from Samson. "The guards are coming!"

"Samson, let go of the bars! We have to go!" Manoah was almost hysterical as his brother pulled him into the shadows.

Just then, something amazing started to happen. The iron bars started to slowly move under Samson's grip.

"It's working, Samson! Keep pulling!" Joel exclaimed. He picked up the small child from his mother's lap and lifted him through the opening in the bars.

Manoah and Asahel stood frozen in the shadows, watching in amazement. The little boy ran to them and hid, waiting breathlessly for his mother to be released.

Samson continued to pull the bars apart, and soon the opening was big enough for the others to climb out. Joel lifted the woman and the old Hebrew man through first; then the others followed. The prisoners squeezed through the opening one at a time with Samson pulling them up to freedom.

"Samson, they've heard you! We have to go now!" Manoah called, when he saw a soldier emerge from the building with a torch in his hand. The soldier shouted when he saw the prisoners escaping, and the other two guards ran out. Asahel and Manoah scooped up the little boy and grabbed the woman by the hand. They ran in the direction of the eastern gate, with the other prisoners scattering behind them. Once everyone else was out, Samson grabbed Joel's hands and pulled him through the opening in the bars, and the two of them ran as fast as they could, with the soldiers yelling and chasing after them.

"Split up and go to the large tree just outside of the eastern gates. Take that road there so you don't have to pass the guards as you leave town," Samson whispered to his cousin as they ran through the crowds gathered outside of Dagon's temple. "God be with you, Joel," he said as they separated.

"He is with me, Samson!" Joel responded happily as he wove down the narrow street. "He sent you, didn't He?"

CHAPTER 18

Samson hid in a darkened doorway until Joel was completely out of sight. When he stepped out onto the street, he almost collided with a Philistine soldier. The man grabbed him roughly and shook him.

"Are you a Hebrew?" he yelled in Samson's face. "What's your name? What are you doing here?"

"I'm Samson, son of Manoah, from the tribe of Dan. I came to town this morning with my family to trade goods, and I got lost," Samson stammered.

The man dragged him over to a group of soldiers who were obviously looking for the runaway captives.

"Is this the Hebrew you were looking for?" the soldier asked his partner as he pushed Samson forward. Samson found himself standing face-to-face with one of the guards from the prison. The man almost laughed when he looked at Samson.

"What is this—some kind of joke?" the guard said.

"You said it was a long-haired Hebrew."

"Yes, but this is only a boy. There's no way this child could have opened those bars. Keep looking!" The guard turned and walked away to continue his search.

"What a waste of time!" the soldier growled. "Find your parents and get out of here."

Samson didn't hesitate. He turned and ran down the now familiar street and headed directly to the broom tree, under which he had left Hannah and the others only a short time earlier. He found that his father and uncle had arrived safely, as well as the old Hebrew man, the woman, and her little boy. The now large group was huddled silently in the darkness, waiting for the rest of their party to arrive. Only Hannah was on her feet, pacing back and forth, trying to comfort her fussy baby.

"Is Joel here yet?" Samson asked breathlessly as he approached the group. One look at Hannah's face told him he wasn't. He sat with the others and drank deeply of the water that was offered to him.

"I heard you bent iron bars, Samson," Joel's brother Caleb whispered. "Maybe there's something to that Nazirite vow after all."

Samson didn't answer. He looked down at his sore hands. There was no light—the group didn't dare light a fire or a torch to attract attention to themselves, but even in the darkness, Samson could see the blisters starting to rise on the palms of both of his hands.

Another man from Mahaneh-dan joined the hushed conversation. "How did you do it, Samson? Did an angel come to you? Did you see Yahweh like your parents did?"

Manoah heard the discussion and hushed the men. "That's enough!" he snapped. "The last thing we need to do is have stories spreading about a little boy with superhuman strength from God."

"But you saw it, too, didn't you, brother?" Uncle Asahel asked, starting to doubt his memory.

"Of course I saw it!" Manoah seemed upset. "Samson bent those bars and single-handedly helped every one of those people escape. If I hadn't seen it with my own eyes . . ." He seemed at a loss for words.

"Father, you're not angry with me, are you?" Samson asked softly.

The silence that followed made Samson's heart sink. When Manoah finally moved closer to his son and put his arm around him, Samson knew it was going to be all right. "No, Samson, I'm not angry with you," he finally replied. "I'm just afraid, that's all. I'm afraid of what will happen when the Philistines find out what you can do. I'm afraid someone will come and take you from us. I'm just afraid, son." Samson wasn't sure, but he thought his father might be crying. "I've been afraid my entire life," Manoah said so softly that Samson wasn't even sure he had spoken at all.

No one was sure how much time had passed. They all sat shivering on the cold ground. Samson leaned against his father, nodding off from time to time until he was startled by the commotion in the group when someone approached from the darkness.

"Don't be alarmed," the voice called softly.

"Joel?" Uncle Asahel called back.

"Yes, it's me, Father. I'm safe."

Everyone rose to their feet and greeted Joel. Hannah was the first one into his arms. She cried openly as he whispered in her ear.

"There's no time for a reunion," Joel said urgently. "The soldiers are still looking for us. They're putting together a search party to go out on horseback as soon as the sun comes up."

"You all can come back to Zorah and stay at my home until the danger has passed," Manoah offered.

"No, Uncle, I'm afraid that will be too dangerous for your family. We must get as far away from Timnah as we can," Joel answered.

The old Hebrew prisoner spoke for the first time. "We have family in the south," he said, standing protectively next to the woman and her son. "We would be honored if you and your wife would travel with us."

"It will be too dangerous for you to travel with women and children at night. We could try to hide you all until the Philistines stop looking," Manoah said.

"You've done so much for us already," Joel replied. "I'm so thankful to all of you for what you've done for me tonight." He looked directly at Samson as he spoke. "But I can't ask you to put yourselves in danger anymore. We will go south and contact you once we are safe. Please pray for us."

Caleb handed Joel a bundle he had been carrying since he left Mahaneh-dan. "I brought you some clothes and food and a little bit of money in case we got you out." He embraced his brother and held him for a moment. "May God go with you."

"We'll see each other again soon," Joel replied, as he gathered his small group together. "I can't wait to see what God has in store for you, my little cousin." He gave Samson one last embrace.

After Joel left with Hannah, the baby, and the other escaped prisoners, the rest of the group separated. It was decided that it would be safest for everyone to return to their homes before the Philistine search party was out in force. Uncle Asahel and his remaining son, Caleb, led their men back to Mahaneh-dan while Samson and his father walked back through the Sorek Valley and up to their hillside home of Zorah. They reached their home shortly before dawn and found Sarai pacing the floor, looking much older than Samson remembered her looking the day before.

"You're safe!" she exclaimed as she raced to the door to greet her men.

Manoah practically collapsed onto a mat on the floor.

"Aren't you going to tell me what happened?" she asked as she knelt down to help her husband take off his sandals.

Manoah and Samson exchanged a secretive glance. "Well," Manoah began, "our son was very brave, and I do believe that God truly is with him."

"What happened? Where are the others?" It was obvious that Sarai couldn't handle much more suspense.

"They're safe, Mother," Samson said. "Joel and Hannah are going south. Uncle Asahel and the others are going home."

"We should get some sleep. We may have Philistine visitors soon. It would be best if everything looks as normal as possible when they get here." Manoah yawned. "But first, we sleep."

Samson agreed completely. He was asleep almost before he could lie down.

CHAPTER 19

By midmorning, there was a bang at the front door that awakened the entire family. Even Samson's younger brothers were groggy from the previous evening's excitement. Manoah opened the door to find a huge Philistine soldier outside with three others behind him searching the property.

"Get everyone outside now!" he yelled at Manoah.

The family scrambled out the door, rubbing the sleep from their eyes.

"Is this everyone?" the soldier bellowed.

Manoah nodded in response. Two of the men went inside the house and Samson could hear them rummaging through his family's belongings. He silently prayed that they wouldn't find the hidden sword.

"You wouldn't happen to know anything about a group of runaway captives would you?" the soldier questioned the family.

"There's no one here but myself, my wife, and our three sons," Manoah replied.

The soldier examined each of them closely. Sarai stood protectively in front of her children with her eyes down. The man roughly grabbed Samson and pulled him away from his mother.

"Why does this one have such long hair?" the soldier growled.

"He has taken a Nazirite vow," Manoah said, stepping forward.

The soldier called for his partners to join him. The two men from the house and the one soldier who was examining the animal enclosure joined him, and they all studied Samson.

"You don't think this is the one, do you?" the man holding Samson asked the other soldiers.

"He's just a boy. There's no way he could have done what they say he did."

"Yes, but he has long hair and he is an Israelite; you can tell by his clothes."

"They said the long-haired man bent iron bars and freed seven captives. There is no way this boy could have done that."

Samson could feel his mother's eyes burning into the back of him. For some reason he was more worried about what she thought at that moment than what the Philistines thought.

"He's just a child!" Manoah stepped closer, trying to draw the attention of the soldiers away from his son.

Everyone seemed to hold their breath for a moment.

"Yeah, he's just a child," the soldier said chuckling. "Go back to your mother, little one." He pushed Samson away.

The men continued searching until they were satisfied that no one was hiding there. When they finally left, Sarai silently began making breakfast. Samson could tell she was trying to process everything she had just heard.

"Maybe we should cut his hair," Manoah said when they all sat down to eat. "It does draw a lot of attention to him."

Sarai gave him a look that could have melted a candle. Then she studied her oldest son. "Was it you, Samson? Did you do what those men said you did?"

Samson nodded slightly and looked down.

"The Lord appeared to us and told us how to raise this boy. How can we ignore those instructions—especially now that we know?" she said to her husband then turned her full attention back to Samson. "You must never cut your hair, do you understand? Now I know what God is going to use you for. These past eight years, I've been waiting and watching; now I know. God has given you a special gift, Samson. You must continue to keep your part of the promise we made with God, and I know He will continue to give you this gift."

"But Sarai . . ." Manoah tried to interrupt.

"No, Manoah. I know you're afraid. I am too. All of God's children have been afraid for far too long now. We don't have to be afraid anymore. Don't you see what God can do for us if we obey Him?" She turned again to her son. "Samson, don't ever stop believing Yahweh's promise to you. Don't ever break your promise to Him. We're all depending on you."

· PART 2 ·

CHAPTER 20

Samson pretended not to listen to his parents as he gathered his clothes for the weeklong trip to celebrate the Feast of Tabernacles in Shiloh. His brothers Elihu and Hosah fought over a cloak that each insisted belonged to him while his youngest brother, Aaron, sat nearby, watching the commotion. Samson tried in vain to hush his twin brothers who, even at nine years of age, still annoyed him as much as they did when they were babies. Finally, he left the small room he shared with his three brothers and slipped closer to his parents, hoping to catch more of their conversation. He could tell by the hushed tones that they were talking about him again.

"He's only thirteen," his father whispered. "I don't think he's ready to marry yet."

"Yes, but look at him, Manoah. He already looks like a full-grown man. We need to find him a wife soon," Sarai replied, as she folded and packed the cloths that would be used as their tents in Shiloh.

Samson tried to stay out of his mother's line of vision. He knew his aging father could hardly see, but his mother's eyes were still sharp. As he tried to crouch out of sight, he wondered to himself why his parents kept having this discussion about his marriage prospects. He knew his mother was right about his appearance—he was already taller than most of the men in his family, and his long hair and unshaven face gave him a wild, manly appearance, but he still felt like a child. Even though he was now responsible for supervising all of his father's flocks with the help of his brothers, he still loved playing games and running through the hills like a child whenever he had a free moment to himself. He couldn't even imagine getting married.

"Perhaps we can find a suitable match for him from my brother's family," Manoah began again.

"Caleb's daughter Martha is lovely," Sarai said, nodding in agreement. "Too bad we didn't think of her sooner. She is to be married at the end of the year. Ah, but her sister Deborah is still available. Let's talk to your brother about it on our way to Shiloh."

Samson couldn't take it anymore. He stood from his hiding place, surprising both of his parents. "I don't want to marry Deborah! She's just a child, and she follows me around like a puppy. Why do I even have to get married at all?"

"You're practically a man, Samson," his father replied as he turned toward the sound of his son's voice. "You must get married and settle down eventually."

"But I don't want to marry anyone from Uncle Asahel's house," Samson whined. He sounded much more like a child than a man.

"Well then, maybe we can find a nice girl in Shiloh. All of the tribes will be there for the Feast of Tabernacles," his mother said.

Samson cringed inwardly. He didn't know why, but he just couldn't stand the thought of marrying a plain, boring Israelite girl. They were all mean or annoying. When he thought of getting married, his mind instantly took him back to his rescue mission in Timnah five years earlier. He often thought of the beautiful Philistine priestess who had helped him find his way out of Dagon's temple and out of the city. Over the years since that visit, he had tried to convince his father that they should do more business in the Philistine city, but his father would not listen. Manoah insisted that it was not safe for Samson to return there under any circumstances. He was sure someone would eventually recognize him as the long-haired boy who had bent metal bars to free the Hebrew captives.

His mother suspiciously watched him as if she could read his thoughts. He knew it was impossible, but still, she seemed to somehow sense his restlessness.

"This year we will find you a wife," she stated simply. "Now finish packing and get the animals gathered together. We will leave for your uncle's house this afternoon and then on to Shiloh in the morning." The deep wrinkles that creased Sarai's forehead when she worried now relaxed, and she smiled at the thought of gathering with fellow believers for the weeklong holiday.

Samson watched her for a moment and thought perhaps it wouldn't be so bad to find a faithful God-fearing girl to marry. Maybe he could be content to live a simple life like his father. He shifted uneasily, knowing inwardly that he somehow needed more.

CHAPTER 21

Samson gathered his father's flock of sheep and goats and led them down the familiar hillside path toward his uncle's house in Mahaneh-dan. His twin brothers walked on either side of their father, assisting him over the rocky terrain, and his youngest brother walked next to their mother, chattering happily. Samson couldn't help but think about how God had blessed their family over the years. Even though the Philistines came regularly to take what they wanted from the herd and small harvest, the family still had more than enough. For every animal the soldiers took, a ewe was ready to birth two more healthy lambs. The small plot of land on which Sarai grew the family vegetables yielded more produce than even her four hungry sons could eat. Even after the Philistines took their portion, there was still more than enough for them. The harvest they had just brought in was the largest Samson had ever seen. He knew it was the Lord's blessing on his family that made them so fruitful. Just looking at his hunched-over parents surrounded by their young children was proof that God was involved.

He was glad his parents had decided to go to Shiloh for the Feast of Tabernacles. According to his father, Samson had attended once as a young child, but he had no memory of it. Even though it was only one day's walk north of their home, it may as well have been on the other side of the country. There just always seemed to be a reason they could not go. When his mother was expecting the twins, his father worried constantly about her health. Then, after they were born, it was too difficult to make the trip with young babies. The birth of little Aaron again delayed their travel plans. His father tried to attend as often as possible to offer sacrifices and pay his tithes, but with his failing eyesight he hadn't even gone to the past few festivals.

But now it seemed that nothing was going to keep the entire family from visiting the Tent of the Lord, which contained the ark of the covenant. Samson's father had told him stories about the precious box that contained the two tablets of stone on which God Himself had written the law. He said the tent is the dwelling place of God on earth—the same tent Moses told the Israelites to erect during their wanderings in the wilderness.

Samson felt a flutter of excitement as he thought about being so close to Yahweh's presence. This year he was old enough to go with his father to the temple to sacrifice an offering for the family. His mother had carefully packed portions of the harvest to be given as food and drink offerings. His father had selected a goat to be given as a burnt offering. Samson was glad he didn't have to choose one of the lambs he had been caring for. The Passover sacrifice only months earlier had been difficult for him. He knew he shouldn't get attached to the animals in his flock, but after spending so much time with them, it was hard not to. He was even a little sad about leaving the flock to be cared for by a hired boy in Mahaneh-dan while the family went to Shiloh.

"There's Mahaneh-dan!" Aaron called as he ran past Samson, interrupting his thoughts. "I'm going to get to Uncle Asahel's house first!"

"No, you're not," Hosah and Elihu shouted in unison as they ran after him.

Samson was annoyed with his brothers for leaving his father alone, but he couldn't scold them unless he ran after them. Instead, he gave his father an arm to hold and whistled for the sheep to follow.

"Thank you, son," Manoah said as he patted Samson's hand. "Let your mother help me so you can get the animals taken care of. Just get them into the enclosure, and the boy your uncle has hired will take care of the rest. I suppose you're free to enjoy your evening. Why don't you go have fun with the other young people? I'm sure they're celebrating now that the harvesting is finished." Sarai joined them and took her husband's hand. "You've been working so hard, you haven't had time to socialize. No wonder you haven't found a wife." Manoah chuckled and playfully pushed his oldest son away. "Go, have fun—just don't stay out too late; we have to leave early tomorrow morning."

Samson obeyed his father but didn't do it willingly. He toyed with the idea of spending the night with the sheep so he could avoid his cousins and their neighbors, but he decided to give them a chance. Maybe he would change his mind about Israelite girls. Maybe there was a nice girl for him here among his people.

CHAPTER 22

The sun was just starting to set when Samson finished tending to his father's animals. He could hear the festivities taking place throughout the town. The harvest had been plentiful in Mahaneh-dan too. As he made his way to his uncle's house, he saw large sheets laid out next to the houses, covered with grapes the size of plums. He assumed they were to be dried in the sun to make raisins. Women sang and laughed as they stomped grapes in large vats to make juice. Others danced through the streets, obviously enjoying the juice that had already been fermented into wine. One young woman bumped into him, sloshing her drink on the front of his cloak.

"Oh, I'm sorry," she giggled. "Here, have a drink. You look tense." She held her cup up to his mouth, but he turned away. He had forgotten how much he disliked the grape harvest in Mahaneh-dan. It seemed like everything was off limits to him. At home, he was more insulated from temptations. His parents rarely had grapes or grape products in the house, and when they did, it was discreetly kept away from him so he wouldn't break his Nazirite vow. But the streets of this town seemed to flow with temptations.

Samson turned from the giggling girl and quickly walked to his uncle's house, hoping to find a quiet place to escape. Unfortunately, when he got there, he found his father and uncle talking and laughing loudly in the courtyard with the rest of the adults. He went to the back of the house to avoid them. He slowed his steps as he came to the darkened apartment that once had belonged to his cousin Joel and his wife, Hannah. There was no light burning in the window, no fire in the oven outside. He sat down by the lonely hearth and pulled his knees up to his chest. It was a warm evening, but he felt a sudden chill as he sat alone in the dirt. He wondered if Joel, Hannah, and their baby daughter were safe. He knew their journey south would have been filled with dangers—especially with Philistine soldiers hounding their every step. It didn't seem likely that they would have gotten far on foot with the soldiers only a day behind on horseback. No one ever talked about Joel or what may have happened to him, but Samson prayed for him often.

"Samson, is that you?" The familiar voice of his cousin Deborah broke into his thoughts. "Why are you sitting here alone? Come join the rest of us."

"I don't really feel like it, Deborah," he replied gloomily.

"You miss Joel, don't you?" she said kindly as she sat down next to him. "We all miss him. My father used to talk about going south to look for him. He said it's his duty as his only living brother. I guess now that it's been so long, everyone has just kind of given up hope." She sighed deeply, and the two sat in silence for a while.

"Samson, do you remember how you used to tell me riddles when I was a little girl? Do you have any more riddles you could tell me?"

"Come on, Deborah, that's kid stuff. I'm not in the mood . . ."

"Pleeeaaase," she begged, sticking her lower lip out just enough to make Samson smile.

"Oh, all right." Samson exaggerated his annoyance. "Here's one: Who is as big as a mountain yet can fit in your heart?"

"That's too easy. It's God, right?"

"OK, then, try this one. Who can make thunder roar yet can speak in the tiniest whisper?"

"Samson, all of your riddles have the same answer!"

"So, what's wrong with that?"

"I guess you're right. God should always be the answer."

Samson smiled and studied his cousin closely. She was only a couple years younger than he, but she still looked like a little girl. She was nothing like the curvaceous Philistine woman in Timnah.

"Deborah," he asked cautiously, "do you ever think about getting married?"

Her face lit up, and her eyes revealed a flash of joy before she quickly caught herself. "Well, yes," she responded, with more reserve than she felt. "My parents have been talking about finding a good match for me, but I think they are waiting until after my sister's wedding."

Samson nodded but said nothing.

"What kind of girl do you want to marry?" she asked, trying to fill in the awkward pause.

"I don't know. I guess someone tall and pretty with silky hair and . . ." He caught the hurt look on his cousin's face and quickly stopped.

"It sounds like you already have someone in mind." Deborah looked down at her sandaled feet.

"Uh, no," he stammered. "It's just this picture I have in my head; it's no one specific. I don't really know who I'm going to marry. I guess I'll just have to wait and see." He stood up and tried to put some space between them. "So, didn't you say there was a party around here? We should probably go. They'll be looking for you."

Deborah rose to her feet and smiled even though her eyes looked unexplainably sad. She led Samson to the door of her father's house. Samson followed, his mind filled with conflicting thoughts.

"Here you are, Samson," she said as they reached the crowded courtyard of her father's house.

"Aren't you going to stay?" he asked, as she turned to go inside.

"No. I suddenly don't feel much like socializing. I'll see you in the morning."

CHAPTER 23

The courtyard used by Deborah's parents was now crowded with what looked like all of the young people of the town. They were obviously enjoying themselves while their parents were around the corner at Uncle Asahel's house. Most of the faces were familiar, but Samson felt like a complete stranger.

When he was just about to leave, a neighbor boy slapped him on the back and put a cup in his hand. "Here you go," he said thickly. "You have to try this year's early crop. I think it's the best one yet."

"Oh, no thanks. I don't drink wine." He tried to hand the cup back, but the boy had already staggered on to someone else. He dumbly held the cup as his eyes scanned the crowd. Most of the people there were his age, some younger, some older. They all seemed to be having a good time talking and laughing. Samson wished he could just relax and let his guard down for a few hours. Then he saw his twin brothers sitting in a corner looking suspicious. With long strides, he walked over to them and grabbed the cup from Elihu's hand.

"What are you two doing here?" he asked, setting the wine on a nearby table.

"Father said we could come for a little while," Elihu protested as he retrieved his cup.

"You're not our boss, Samson," Hosah interjected. "And just because you can't have wine doesn't mean we can't." He took a long drink from the cup he had been hiding behind his back.

"You're just a child, and besides, you know that stuff isn't good for you. If you want to drink juice, fine, I'll find you some, but don't drink the kind that's fermented."

"Look around, Samson; everyone else is drinking. What's the big deal?"

"Yes, and look how silly they're acting. Do you really want to be like them?"

"You just need to relax, big brother," Elihu said, as he took a drink and pulled his twin away. "Have a little fun! It will be good for you."

"Yeah," Hosah joined in. "You're always so serious."

Samson plopped down where his brothers had been sitting. A girl with a tray of food glided over to him and knelt down next to him.

"Would you like something to eat?" she asked as she held the tray out to him.

It was filled with an assortment of plump red and green grapes. "Don't you have anything else?" he asked, beginning to feel overwhelmed.

"You're in Mahaneh-dan just days after the grape harvest, silly. What did you expect?" She giggled and stood up. "There may be some bread over there if you'd like," she said pointing to a table nearby. "Just help yourself, and hey—relax and have fun. It's a party!" She smiled and spun in a graceful circle toward a group of boys standing nearby.

Samson walked to the table of food and selected a few small loaves of bread and a handful of fresh figs. As he reached for the tray of newly harvested cucumbers, he spotted his cousin Martha for the first time.

She danced seductively for a small group that had gathered in a corner to watch her. Three other girls played tambourines nearby. Samson watched from a distance for a while, but he found himself being pulled closer to the music. Martha spun and swayed, first slowly then faster and faster as the tambourines changed their rhythm. Samson's heart pounded with the beat of the song, and he stood mesmerized by Martha's beauty and grace. When the dance ended, the audience cheered wildly while Samson stood dazed. Martha smiled and accepted the drink a young man offered her. She seemed to feel Samson's eyes on her, and she walked boldly over to him.

"Did you like my dance, Samson?" she asked breathlessly.

"Yes," he stammered. "You looked beautiful."

"Would you like to go for a walk with me?"

He couldn't speak, so he nodded and followed her away from the crowd. As they walked in silence, his mind replayed all the cruel things she had said to him over the years. He wondered how she would treat him without an audience to laugh at her barbs. He realized he had never been alone with her, and he suddenly felt afraid.

Once they were away from the noise, she spoke. "I've heard stories about you, Samson, and I've always wondered if they are true." Her voice sounded like tinkling bells. "I heard that Joel taught you how to be a warrior when you were just a little boy." She stopped walking and turned to face him. Her skin seemed to glow in the moonlight. "I heard you bent metal bars with your bare hands. You were just a child then, but now you look like a man. How is it that you are younger than me, but you look so grown up?" She took a sip from her cup. "If you could do all those things when you were a boy, what kind of things can you do now that you're a man?"

"I don't know," he replied shyly. "Maybe those are just stories. What makes you think they're true?"

"You're right; they probably are just made up. People around here don't have much to occupy their time. They have nothing better to do than make up stories about little boys." She held her cup up to Samson's mouth, and he drank without thinking. The thick, sweet liquid covered his tongue and slid down his throat, leaving a trail of warmth all the way down. He hesitated, but didn't feel anything unusual. His entire life he had felt that if he broke his Nazirite vow in any way, he would be punished instantly—perhaps a bolt of lightning would strike him dead, or the ground would open up and swallow him. But nothing happened when he drank the wine. He took the cup from Martha's hand and drank the rest of the wine in one swallow. He instantly felt lighter.

"There now, that's better," Martha cooed. "You're finally having fun. We'd better get back. I'm practically a married woman. I could get in trouble being out here alone with you." She smiled playfully and walked back toward the noise of the crowd. Samson trailed behind, filled with a strange mixture of relief and disappointment.

CHAPTER 24

The next morning, Samson peeled his eyes open and looked around the strange room, not instantly recognizing that he was in his uncle's house. He tried to lift his head from the sleeping mat, but it was too heavy. He closed his eyes and moaned as the memories of the previous night came flooding back to him.

"Get up," he heard his father snap from the doorway.

Samson tried to speak, but his mouth felt like it was full of wool, and his jaw was unexplainably sore.

"You were drinking," his father stated. It obviously wasn't a question.

Samson sat up too quickly, causing his stomach to lurch.

"Where is everyone?" he whispered as the sound of his own voice boomed in his head.

"They're preparing to leave for Shiloh. Did you forget that we are going to celebrate the holy week at the Tabernacle of God?" Samson did not miss the edge in his father's voice. "Get up and wash yourself and get the goat for the sacrifice. And don't let your mother see you like this." He turned and walked out, leaving Samson alone.

He held his head in his hands for a few moments until his stomach settled down enough for him to move. *Why did I do this to myself?* he asked himself miserably. As he walked outside to the well, he had to pass by the family members and neighbors who were all busy loading carts and donkeys for the trip north. He felt as though everyone was staring at him. His mind replayed what had happened after he returned to the party with Martha. Once he started with the first sip of wine, it became too easy to continue with cup after cup of the sweet, intoxicating liquid. He found himself relaxing and talking more easily to the other party guests, but eventually he started talking too much. He cringed as he remembered all the foolish things he had said to his cousin, Martha. He told her she was beautiful and that he loved her. He may have even said something about marrying her.

He reached the well and splashed cold water on his face, trying to wash away the embarrassment. The fact that Martha was betrothed to another man had never crossed Samson's mind as he showered her with praise and adoration, that is, until her fiancé joined the party. Samson rubbed his sore jaw as the memories slowly came back to him. He remembered a man tapping him on the shoulder and introducing himself as Martha's fiancé. Samson had a few choice words for the man, but that was put to a quick end when he felt one punch to the chin that knocked him flat on his back. The pulsing strength that Samson had felt at various times in his life was completely numbed by the wine. Instead of getting up to fight back, he just lay there on the floor until he was carried to bed.

Samson pulled another bucket of water from the well and dunked his entire head in it, trying to drown the memories. He jumped when he felt someone tap him on the back. He raised his head from the bucket and stood face-to-face with Martha's younger sister, Deborah. He felt an unexplainable guilt wash over him.

"Your father sent me to find you," she said coldly without making eye contact. "The family is ready to leave." She turned to walk away, but Samson grabbed her arm.

"Wait," he pleaded desperately. "Were you there last night? You didn't see me, did you?"

"No, I was helping our mothers and the other women prepare for the trip. I was not there and I did not see you, but I heard plenty."

"Deborah, I didn't mean any of what I said to your sister."

"Didn't you?"

"It was the wine. I've never had a drop to drink before, and I guess I just couldn't handle myself." He didn't know why he felt he had to explain himself to this girl.

"What about your vow, Samson? How could you just forget about the promise you made to God—after all these years?" She looked noticeably upset. "I just thought you were stronger than that." Without another word, she turned and walked toward the crowd that had gathered to leave.

Samson didn't know what to do. He was too ashamed to even pray for guidance. Then he remembered he had to get his father's goat. He entered the animal enclosure where all of the town's goats and sheep were being kept during the holiday week. He quickly spotted the young goat that his father planned to take to Shiloh. Then from the corner of his eye, he saw his favorite little ewe lamb. Her mother had had trouble birthing her, so Samson was there caring for her right from the beginning of her life. In spite of her difficult beginnings, she was a perfect animal. She was also much tamer than the others. She seemed to know that Samson saved her life, so she followed him around like a pet.

Samson knelt down and the lamb came right to him. He stroked her soft wool, and she nibbled on the corner of his cloak. He suddenly realized what he had to do. He knew that he had sinned, but deep down he also knew that he could have forgiveness. His father had taught him that the blood of a lamb could cover sins. As much as he hated to sacrifice his beloved pet, he hated even more feeling separated from God.

He found a strap of leather and a small bell that he fastened around his lamb's neck so he could keep track of her.

"Come on, little friend. You and I have a trip to take."

CHAPTER 25

Shiloh, the spiritual capital of Israel, was only a day's travel away from Mahaneh-dan, but to Samson it felt as if the journey would never end. The late-summer sun beat down on his head, intensifying the pounding that occurred every time he took a step. He was unable to eat breakfast, so, as the day wore on, he began to feel light-headed and weak. His mother thought he was sick, so she tried to care for him by giving him extra water and food along the way, but Samson moodily shrugged her off, preferring to avoid her curious stares. His usually rowdy brothers appeared to be dragging as well, so the three of them walked together in silent misery. When the group stopped at midday to eat and rest under a grove of shade trees, Samson curled up alone with a hard loaf of bread and a handful of olives. As he ate, he started to feel a little better. The waves of nausea eventually eased, and the drumming in his head dulled to a soft but steady thumping. He closed his eyes and leaned his head back against the trunk of the tree.

"How's your jaw?" It was Martha standing in front of him, nibbling on a chunk of cheese.

"It's a little sore," he admitted rubbing his bearded chin.

"I'm sorry about last night. I didn't think the wine would affect you so badly." Not waiting for an invitation, she sat down next to him.

"I had no business drinking it at all," he said sullenly. "And all those stupid things I said to you—you know I didn't mean them, right?"

She nodded and looked down. "Merab was pretty angry." She laughed without humor.

"Merab, is that his name? At least you know your husband has a good right punch," Samson replied.

"I guess I thought you would have a little more fight in you. The stories I've heard . . ." her voice trailed off.

The realization that Martha had manipulated and used him finally sunk in. "You got me drunk and led me on, knowing that your fiancé would have to fight for you."

"I didn't make you do anything." Martha looked offended. "I simply offered you something to drink and you took it! If Merab happened to show up when you were pawing all over me, that's not my fault." She stood up and brushed off the back of her robe. "You're a big boy, Samson. You can't blame me for your actions." Her eyes revealed her disdain. "What a disappointment you turned out to be." She turned and walked away.

Samson felt awful. He was a disappointment—to his father, to himself, but mostly to God. He pulled out his dagger from the strap around his thigh and gathered his long hair together in the other hand. He thought about his Nazirite vow, how it had always made him an outsider. *Last night was the first time I felt comfortable with my peers. I liked having fun for a little while. I enjoyed being able to relax without the expectations of my family and the uncertainty of God's plans always looming over me like a storm cloud. I already broke my vow by drinking wine. I might just as well cut off my hair and show the world that I'm not God's special Nazirite anymore.* He held the blade at the nape of his neck while squeezing his eyes shut tightly and holding his breath. That's when he heard a small sound in the distance that made him open his eyes and put down the dagger. It was the little bell he had fastened around his lamb's neck. The animal was off in the distance playing with some of the younger children. They laughed and squealed as the lamb bounded around after them.

"Forgiveness," Samson whispered aloud to himself. Tears sprang to his eyes, and he put the dagger back in its sheath. "I know I don't deserve it, God, but will You please forgive me? Please help me to do better. Help me keep my part of our covenant. I can't do it without You." Somewhere deep down, he knew God didn't want his hair—only his heart. He could never undo the wrongs that he had done, but he knew if he was willing, God could still use him. Feeling lighter and stronger, Samson rose to his feet to finish the journey to Shiloh.

Chapter 26

The group continued traveling north throughout the entire day, growing more tired and quiet. As evening approached, Samson could see lights off in the distance.

"What is that?" he asked his father, who was riding a donkey beside him.

"I can't see as far as you can, son, but if you're talking about the lights, that is Shiloh." He squinted in the general direction of the town. "All week long the young men will climb ladders carrying pitchers of oil to refill the lamps and keep the flames burning."

"I see tents everywhere. It's beautiful," Samson said with awe in his voice.

"The Feast of Tabernacles is one of my favorite celebrations. It is a wonderful holiday filled with music and festivities, but it's also a reminder of where our people came from," Manoah explained.

"What do you mean?" Samson's three younger brothers had gathered closer to their father so they could hear the explanation too.

"We'll live and eat in a tent all week to remind us of our ancestors who wandered through the wilderness for forty years before settling here in the Promised Land."

"It's like camping," Samson's youngest brother, Aaron, exclaimed.

"Oh, it's more than just camping," Manoah chuckled. "We could put a tent up anywhere, but Shiloh is a special place. This is where God dwells with people."

The boys were all silent for a few moments.

"Will we get to see Him?" Elihu finally asked.

"Perhaps," Manoah answered. "Keep your eyes on the tabernacle. If you see a heavy cloud around it, that is God's presence." He urged his donkey to walk faster. "Come on, boys," he called over his shoulder. "If we hurry, we can make it to the evening service!"

They all ran to catch up. The rest of the family quickened their pace as well. The closer they got to the town, the more tents they saw dotting the landscape. Hundreds of families had already set up camp.

"Manoah, let's stop here," Sarai called to her husband. "If we go much closer, it will be too crowded."

"Very well," he answered as he slid off the donkey. "Brother, what do you think of this spot?" he asked Asahel.

"It's perfect! Let's set up camp so we can get to the tabernacle before dark."

The family sprung into action, unloading carts and packs. With surprising efficiency, they erected two large tents—one for the men and one for the women. The young children gathered wood, and the women began making a fire and preparing the evening meal.

"Samson, get the goat. I think we can still make it," Manoah called to his son when the work was finished.

"Father, I have something to ask you," Samson began hesitantly. "May I give my lamb as a sin offering instead?"

"But you love that lamb . . ." Manoah began but then slowly nodded in understanding. "Yes, son, I think that is a good idea. You saved that lamb, so it rightfully belongs to you. You may choose to give it as a sin offering."

Samson easily found the animal and lifted it onto his shoulders. He took his father's arm and led him into the town of Shiloh. The closer they got to the tabernacle, the more crowded the streets became. Samson could smell burning meat mixed with incense. He saw a group of young women dancing in the street. It wasn't at all like the dance Martha had done at the party to draw attention to herself. These girls were obviously dancing to celebrate and honor God. Samson paused for a moment to watch them.

"Maybe your mother is right," Manoah muttered. "We really should find you a wife."

Samson blushed and hurried away from the girls.

"There it is." Samson stood in awe outside the entrance to the tabernacle. There was a short line leading to the bronze altar where a priest was conducting the evening sacrifices. The mood in and around the outer courtyard was much more solemn than in the streets. Barefoot men in pure white robes wove through the crowds, carrying out their designated tasks. Samson could see the high priest at the altar. He wore an ephod embedded with precious stones over his chest and a tall white turban on his head. The line moved quickly, and soon Samson and Manoah were standing face-to-face with the high priest.

"Ah, a Nazirite," the man greeted them warmly. "What is your name, son?"

"I'm Samson and this is my father, Manoah. We're from Zorah," he answered politely.

"*Hmmm,* Samson son of Manoah . . . where have I heard that name before?" He scratched his thick dark beard, obviously trying to retrieve a long-buried memory. "Ah well. I can't seem to remember." He shook his head and smiled. "What did you bring for an offering?"

Samson placed his lamb on the altar. "I would like to give her as a sin offering," Samson said in a shaky voice.

The priest stepped back, and Samson placed both of his hands on the lamb's head. He whispered his sins up to God, symbolically transferring his transgressions onto the animal. He then took his knife and killed his pet lamb. While Samson's tears flowed freely into his beard, the priest took the animal and separated it. Some parts of the lamb were burned while others were set aside for the priests.

"I know it's hard," the priest said kindly. "But your sins are now covered. Go on your way and sin no more."

Samson could only nod and sniff like a child.

Manoah took his son's arm, and the two left the courtyard of the tabernacle. "It isn't as much fun as you thought it would be, is it?" he asked softly. "Sometimes we're in such a hurry to try new things and to be an adult that we don't realize how difficult it can be."

"I'm so sorry, Father," Samson cried. "I let everyone down."

"No. You made a mistake. Don't think for a moment that God won't be able to use you now." Manoah patted his son's hand. "Sometimes in our weakness and frailty, God finds His greatest strength."

Samson hid the words in his heart in case he needed them later. Somehow he knew he would.

CHAPTER 27

The tent the men shared at night was crowded, but after the long day of walking, everyone was tired. Samson slept peacefully and woke feeling surprisingly refreshed the next morning. He was one of the last to awaken, so he quickly dressed and joined his family outside. He found the women talking happily as they prepared the morning meal. Children chased each other through the campsites, careful to avoid the cooking pits. Several of the men had gone to the city gates to listen to the elders, so Samson decided to go find them. As he walked through the maze of tents, he saw his father, who was having a heated discussion with Deborah and Martha's father. He was about to walk away when he heard his name. He wondered why they were talking about him, so he crept closer, hoping no one would notice him.

"I just don't understand why you're being so stubborn about this, Caleb!" Manoah exclaimed. Even from a distance, Samson could see his father's face was red, and his fists were clenched. "After everything Samson did for your brother Joel, I can't believe you would refuse to give him your daughter."

"Deborah is my youngest and my favorite. She's not as pretty as her sister, but I believe we can do better for her." Caleb saw the anger rising in the older man's face and quickly tried to recover. "I don't mean any disrespect, Uncle Manoah, it's just . . ."

"It's just what? He's a good boy!"

"Yes, but . . ."

"But what?"

"He's—"

"What, Caleb? Say it!"

"He's strange!" Caleb finally blurted out but seemed to instantly regret his choice of words.

Manoah's face changed color yet again. "He's a Nazirite! He's not strange. God chose him to be a Nazirite."

"Yes, and he broke the Nazirite vow right outside my home the night before last. How can I trust him to keep a covenant with my daughter if he can't even keep one with God?"

Manoah exhaled slowly and hung his head. "He made a mistake. Don't you think he deserves a second chance?"

"I'm sorry, Uncle. I just . . ."

Samson didn't stay around to hear the rest of the conversation. He quickly turned and walked toward the tabernacle, clenching his fists and grinding his teeth. He didn't want to marry Deborah anyway. She was just a baby! He couldn't think of a single girl in the entire country that he would want to have as a wife. If they were all as judgmental as Deborah and manipulative as Martha, he didn't want anything to do with any of them.

When he reached the tabernacle, he slowed down and tried to calm his pounding heart. He moved toward the opening of the outer court and casually watched the priests inside. They seemed so content serving God. He wished he were a Levite so he could work at the tabernacle. Just then, a voice interrupted his brooding thoughts.

"Nazirite, come here."

Samson turned and saw the high priest calling. He looked over his shoulder to make sure there wasn't another long-haired man standing behind him before he was sure the priest was talking to him. He blushed slightly and walked to the older man.

"You're Samson, son of Manoah, from Zorah, right?"

"Yes."

The priest grinned, obviously very pleased with himself. "Do you have a relative named Joel?"

"Yes, yes!" Samson exclaimed, barely able to contain himself. "He's my cousin. Have you seen him?"

"It's been a couple years, but yes, he was here for Passover with his family. He had a wife and two young children, I believe."

"Did he tell you where he's living?"

"No, he just said he is staying with friends in the south. I think he was hoping to find his family here, but when he didn't, he asked me to remember him in case you ever came." The man smiled as he remembered something. "He told me about a little Nazirite boy named Samson whom

God used to help him escape from the Philistines, and now here you are." His smile grew wider. "It's been many years since we've had a deliverer."

"I'm no deliverer," Samson replied, feeling embarrassed.

"That's not what I heard. I've been praying for a long time. Praying and waiting and watching—and now, here you are."

"Yes, but what am I supposed to do? My own family doesn't even trust me. What kind of leader will I be if those closest to me won't even follow?"

"Well, maybe God doesn't plan on using your family. Maybe He has something else in mind for you. Just be still and listen. You will know what Yahweh wants you to do."

Samson nodded. "There have been times when I was sure I knew His will. I could almost feel Him moving me, but it's been so long." He looked into the kind eyes of the priest, hoping he could help supply answers. "What if God doesn't want me anymore? What if He changed His mind?"

"God doesn't change His mind." The priest smiled. "Just be still and listen, my boy. You will know soon enough what God has planned for you." He patted Samson on the shoulder and went back into the tabernacle, smiling as though he knew a secret.

Samson couldn't help but feel better after his talk with the priest. Joel was alive and well! He felt certain that somehow everything else would fall into place.

CHAPTER 28

The family rejoiced when they heard the news about Joel. Any hard feelings between Manoah and his nephew, Caleb, were soon erased, or at least hidden well. Samson spent most of his time at the tabernacle, watching the daily routine of the priests, or at the city gates, listening to the elders discuss various issues. Each evening there was celebrating and feasting with every family sharing what they had with their neighbors. It was a wonderful week without even a single Philistine soldier to darken the festivities.

Once all the tents were taken down and the crowds began to disperse, Samson felt an unexplainable sadness. Again he wished he could work at the tabernacle or find some other occupation in Shiloh. He knew deep down that he was not made to be a shepherd like his father, but he still didn't know what he was supposed to do.

During the journey home, Samson was quiet. His mother hovered and worried, but his father seemed to understand that he just needed some time to think. After spending a night in Mahaneh-dan and gathering the animals that belonged to them, Manoah led his family back home to Zorah. They all seemed to sense that something had changed. That evening at dinner, while Samson was gathered with his parents and brothers, he made the announcement he had been rehearsing in his mind all day.

"I'm leaving home," he said simply. It nearly broke his heart to see the tears that welled in his mother's eyes.

"Where will you go, son?" his father asked.

"I think I will try to find Joel. If I travel south and ask around, I'm sure to find out something about him."

"But who will look after you?" his mother sobbed.

CHAPTER 28

Manoah placed his hand on his wife's shoulder. "Samson is a man now; he can look after himself." He lovingly brushed away her tears. "There now, you can't expect him to live here with us forever."

"I guess I just thought he would get married and we would add on a room for him and his family and . . ." Her voice trailed off.

"We've always known our Samson was set aside for something else."

Samson's brothers were surprisingly quiet as they watched the scene. It almost seemed that they, too, were sad to see him go. For a moment, Samson considered staying, but he knew he would never be satisfied in the hills of Zorah. Without another word, he went to the room he shared with his brothers and began packing.

His father entered the room carrying a large bundle. He laid it on the floor in front of Samson.

"What is it?" he asked.

"It's the sword Joel gave you, as well as some money I had hidden away. You may need both on your journey."

"Thank you, Father," he said as he kissed the old man on both cheeks. "I plan to leave before dawn tomorrow. Will you please tell mother? I just can't . . ."

"Yes, son, I'll tell her. She's already preparing more food than even you will be able to carry," Manoah chuckled. He straightened his hunched shoulders and for a moment looked stronger than he had in years. "May God go with you, Samson."

After his father left the room, Samson pulled the large iron sword from the bundle. It felt much lighter than it had the last time he had held it.

"What's that?" his brother Elihu asked from the doorway.

"It belonged to a Philistine soldier. Cousin Joel killed the man and gave the sword to me to use for training. I didn't have nearly enough time to really learn how to use it."

"May I hold it?" Elihu asked in awe.

Samson handed the sword to his younger brother, who nearly dropped it. "It's a lot heavier than it looks," Elihu said.

Samson continued packing while his brother swished the sword in the air. "I hope you don't need to use this," Elihu said.

"Yeah, me too."

Elihu handed the sword back to Samson, who returned it to its bundle.

"Are you scared, Samson?"

"Of what?" Samson answered, sounding braver than he felt. "I'm not looking for trouble, I'm just looking for Joel."

Elihu laughed. "Yes, but you may find both."

"I don't know. I guess I'm more worried about leaving all of you out here alone in the hills. You never know when the Philistines will come pounding on the door."

"Don't worry. I'll look after everyone while you're gone. I'm pretty strong, too, you know." Elihu flexed his muscles to prove his point.

Samson chuckled and gave his brother a playful shove. "I have something for you," he said, getting more serious. He walked to the corner where he kept the shepherd staff his father had given him when he was a child. He held it out to his brother but didn't say a word.

"But Samson, this is your favorite . . ."

"Yeah, but I don't think I'll need it anymore. Besides, I need you to take care of the flock while I'm gone." They both knew he meant more than just the sheep.

"Well, I'd better get some rest. I'm going to leave early tomorrow. I guess I'll see you later," Samson said, trying to sound casual.

Elihu gave his older brother a quick and awkward hug then turned to leave. "Yeah, I'll see you," he called over his shoulder. "I'm going to stay up for a while. I'll tell the other boys to leave you alone so you can get some rest."

Samson sighed and plopped down on his sleeping mat. As crazy as his family made him feel sometimes, he was thankful for all of them.

He laid his head down and tried to sleep, knowing he would need his rest for the long journey ahead.

CHAPTER 29

Samson had every intention of going south to find Joel, but when he left his home early the next morning, something pulled him toward Timnah. He hadn't been to the Philistine town in more than five years, but for some reason, he wanted to go back.

He reached the city gates just as the guards were opening them. He knew he could find a way in through the side streets, but instead, he waited with the other merchants and visitors until he was allowed to enter legally. He felt as though the soldiers that surrounded the gates were eying him suspiciously, but no one stopped him.

When he reached the market, he wandered from booth to booth, looking at the strange and wonderful goods that came from all over the country. Vendors shouted to get the attention of the buyers as they passed by, but it wasn't the shouting that got Samson's attention. Two beautiful young women stood quietly behind a booth that displayed grapes and raisins. They whispered to one another, oblivious to the noisy crowd. Samson watched from a distance as they giggled and smiled. He wondered what they were talking about that made them so happy. He found himself smiling just watching them. Then a tall older man approached and scolded the girls. He must have been their father. The girls immediately got to work, talking to anyone who even hesitated in front of their stand. Samson was about to move in closer when he heard someone calling his name. He looked around but didn't see anyone he knew.

"It is you!" a young man standing right in front of him exclaimed. "Look at all that hair!"

"Do I know you?" Samson asked, feeling very confused and flustered.

"You don't remember your own cousin? It's me, Alvah!" He put up his fists and pretended to jab a few punches at Samson. "You're not still mad at me, are you?"

"You mean for turning Joel in to the Philistines?" Samson responded, feeling his face turn red. "Well, I don't know how you forgive a person for something like that."

"Come on. I heard he got away. The Philistines gave up looking for him years ago. No harm done!" Alvah moved in closer and talked in a mock whisper. "You didn't have anything to do with helping him escape, did you?" He didn't wait for a response. "That's all right; I know it was you. Who else could it have been? A superstrong Hebrew with long hair—that has 'Samson' written all over it!" Alvah put his hand on his cousin's shoulder and led him to the booth that he had been studying. "You should know I never told the Philistines it was you. I could have, you know. I could have told them where you live and everything, but I would never do that to you. After all, we are family."

Samson didn't buy Alvah's overfriendly act for a minute. There was no way he was going to trust this traitor after everything he had done. Sure it had been years and they were just children, but he had betrayed Joel! How could he ever be forgiven for that? Samson found himself standing right in front of the girls he had been watching. Alvah must have read something in his expression because he laughed and patted Samson on the back.

"Samson, I'd like you to meet Peles and her younger sister Metsor. Their father owns a large vineyard just outside of town."

"Hello," Peles answered politely. "Would you like to try some of our grapes? People say they're the best in the region." She was without a doubt the most beautiful young woman he had ever seen. He found himself staring openly at her suntanned face and full pink lips. Her head was uncovered, revealing a mane of glistening light-brown hair that looked as though it were woven with strands of gold. She held her small hand out to him revealing a palm full of deep purple grapes. He started to reach out his hand, but he quickly caught himself.

"No, thank you. I must be going," he answered curtly.

"I'm sorry about my friend," Alvah answered, looking embarrassed. "He's not from around here."

The younger girl giggled. "That's obvious. Just look at him; he looks like a wild man from the wilderness."

CHAPTER 29

Her sister silenced her with an elbow jab and looked at Samson apologetically.

"I have to go," Samson stammered as he quickly walked away from the group. Alvah was right behind him.

"What's wrong with you?" he asked, taking two steps for every one of Samson's. "Haven't you ever seen a girl before?"

Samson turned to face his cousin. "What are you doing here, Alvah?"

"I live here, remember? Look, I work right over there at the ironsmith shop. I'm an apprentice."

"You make weapons that are used to kill your own people?" Samson asked in amazement.

"No. We make mostly farm tools," Alvah answered indignantly. "We sell them to *everyone,* even Israelites." Samson started to walk away, but Alvah grabbed him roughly by the shoulders. "Hey, what's your problem? Do you really mean to tell me you can't get over something that happened more than five years ago? I've forgiven you for breaking my nose! I'm not holding a grudge against you and all those hypocrites back in Mahaneh-dan." Samson couldn't tell if he was sincere, but for some reason he couldn't make himself walk away. "Look, I'm just trying to live my life, Samson! I made a mistake. I'm sorry. Haven't you ever done something you regret?"

Samson sighed and dropped his shoulders. "Yeah. I've made mistakes," he said softly. "I guess I do appreciate you not telling the Philistines about me. But what you did to Joel . . ."

"But he's alive, isn't he?" Alvah retorted.

"Yes, he's alive. I'm going to look for him as soon as I leave Timnah."

"Why don't you stay here for a while? It's really not so bad. The people here have been kind to my mother and me. We've finally found a place where we fit in. Maybe you'll like it here too."

"I can't stay. I don't even know why I came here."

"At least come to my house so I can share a meal with you. I don't have to be back to work until later this afternoon. My mother will be happy to see you." Alvah led Samson through the crowded streets to a little house behind the ironsmith shop. Samson reluctantly followed.

Once inside, he began to relax with Alvah and his mother. They talked about family and familiar places. It didn't take long for Samson to completely let his guard down. Alvah seemed harmless enough.

After the meal, Alvah rose and said he had to go to work.

101

"I have to be on my way too," Samson said as he stood to leave. "Thank you for the meal."

Samson walked with his cousin to the ironsmith shop. "I'm sorry about how things turned out between us, Alvah."

"Me too." His response sounded sincere. "You know, it's not too late to change your mind about going south. I'm sure Joel is just fine. You could stay here and get to know some of the locals—maybe even those girls in the market." He laughed and slapped the blushing Samson on the back.

"No, I really need to find Joel. I want to see for myself that he is safe."

"All right. I hope you find what you're looking for," Alvah replied. "May Dagon guide you," he called as Samson was already walking away.

Samson cringed inwardly but didn't respond.

CHAPTER 30

Samson had considered himself well traveled. After all, he had spent several years taking his father's herd to pasture lands throughout the region. But now that he wasn't tied down to a flock of sheep, he had much more freedom to travel through the Philistine cities that his father was always careful to avoid.

After leaving Timnah, Samson traveled south to a larger Philistine city called Ashkelon. He walked the beautiful sandy beaches and watched as wealthy young men strutted through the streets wearing fine linen robes. He wondered how men his age were able to afford such expensive clothes. It didn't take long for him to find out.

On his first evening in Ashkelon, he sat on the beach watching the sun sink into the sea. He decided it would be a good place to camp, so he built a small fire and leaned his back against a palm tree. He opened his pack and pulled out a loaf of bread his mother had sent. Seeing the lovingly packed food made him just a little bit homesick.

Before the sun was completely down, Samson saw a young Philistine man walking toward him on the beach. He was clean shaven and had short hair, which made him look like a young boy from a distance. When he got closer, Samson could see he was probably about his age though quite a bit smaller.

"Hello," the young man called as he approached. "You're not from around here, are you?"

"Is it that obvious?" Samson smiled.

The man introduced himself as Saph and invited Samson to come meet his friends. Samson agreed, banked his fire, and gathered his belongings. As the two walked, the contents of his pack clanged together and attracted the attention of the young Philistine.

"What do you have in there?"

"Just a few things I brought from home."

"It looks heavy. Can I see?"

Samson hesitated for a moment, but the man seemed trustworthy enough. He opened the pack and revealed the handle of his sword.

"Wow, that's some weapon you've got there. Where did you get it?" Saph asked, obviously impressed.

"My cousin gave it to me when I was a child."

Saph touched the engraved handle reverently. "That's the weapon of a Philistine soldier. I should know; my father has one just like it."

Samson's heart fluttered in his chest, and he knew at once he had made a mistake trusting this young man.

"That's interesting," Samson said cautiously. "Like I said, my cousin gave it to me. Maybe he bought it from a soldier."

"I doubt that." Saph still smiled casually. "Soldiers don't sell their weapons." He shrugged and continued on his way. "Oh, well. What do I care? It's not like I've never taken anything that didn't belong to me." He laughed and Samson let out his breath.

Saph led Samson to a courtyard filled with young men and women. They were dancing and laughing. Everyone greeted Samson warmly, and he felt a little more comfortable with each passing minute. Saph offered him a drink, but he hesitated.

"I don't drink wine," he explained.

"Oh, this isn't wine. It's camel's milk. We sweeten it with special spices."

Samson smelled the drink and it seemed fine, so he took a small sip. It was warm and thick and instantly made him feel relaxed.

He enjoyed the company of the young Philistines. They didn't seem to care that he looked different or that his clothes weren't as nice. They shared what they had with him, keeping his cup and his plate full. Before long, he found himself getting extremely tired. He told Saph he was going back to his camp on the beach, but everyone insisted he stay. He decided to rest on a cushion for just a few minutes; then he would leave. His eyes were so heavy that he just couldn't keep them open any longer.

When he woke, the sun was up and the courtyard was empty. The only thing that remained from the night before was the cushion he had slept on and the empty cup he held in his hand. Even his pack was gone. The Philistines had taken everything—his clothes, food, money, and

Joel's sword. He threw the cup across the courtyard then stood to his feet. Pushing his hand through his now loose hair, he began pacing. *What was I thinking? How could I have trusted those Philistines?* He kicked the cushion at his feet than collapsed back onto the ground. He considered trying to get his belongings back, but he knew it would be impossible to reclaim the Philistine sword. No one would believe it was rightfully his. Saph and his friends were nothing but criminals, but they were sons of soldiers, and he was a lone Hebrew in a strange city. Besides, he was only one man. What could he do against so many? It didn't take him long to decide to get out of Ashkelon as quickly as possible. He knew it was time to travel back into the lands where his people lived, people he could trust. He was sure once he got into Judah, he could find a way to get food. Maybe he would even be able to find Joel.

CHAPTER 31

From Ashkelon, Samson headed inland to the Judean town of Debir. There a family took him in and fed him, but they seemed to do so out of obligation rather than true kindness. Samson didn't stay long. Next, he traveled to the hilltop town of Hebron, asking people along the way if they knew Joel and Hannah. Few people made eye contact with him, and even fewer spoke. Every place he went, the people seemed afraid and withdrawn. When he arrived in a little village called Lehi, he finally got a lead. A woman at the well told him to go to the home of Simeon, which Samson found without much searching. A boy a few years younger than Samson answered the door.

"I'm looking for Simeon," Samson began politely. "I'm hoping to find information about my cousin, Joel."

Samson thought he caught a dark shadow flash across the boy's eyes. Before he could ask more questions, an old man emerged from the house and greeted Samson warmly.

"My, my, just look how much you've grown." He held out his hand and welcomed him in.

After washing Samson's feet and offering him food and water, the old man and the boy sat across from Samson and stared at him intently. "It's good to see you again, my boy," the man said.

"Have we met before?" Samson asked, feeling a bit embarrassed.

"I'm sure you don't recognize me. We only met once and it was dark, but I know you. You saved my life. You pulled me and my daughter and my grandson here out of that Philistine pit."

"So, you were the family that escaped with Joel!" Samson exclaimed, finally remembering who they were.

"Yes, and now you've come to find him. Oh, I wish I had better news for you. If only you'd come a year earlier . . ." Simeon's voice broke.

Samson felt a sick knot of dread form in his stomach. "What happened to him?"

"Well, when we left Timnah, we knew the Philistines were close behind us. We knew we couldn't outrun them, so we hid in a cave in the Rock of Etam for several days until we had to venture out to find food and water. We came here to see if it was safe. The people were kind and took us all in and hid us whenever the Philistines passed through looking for us. As time went on, the soldiers came less and less frequently. Eventually, I think they gave up. Things were good for a while. Joel traveled through the land of Judah, trying to assemble an army to stand up to the Philistines. He rallied thousands of men who said they were ready to fight. Feeling confident that the south was secure, Joel went as far north as Shiloh and tried to gather men along the way, but he did not have as much success there. When he came back, his army had begun to disintegrate without their leader. Somehow the Philistines had heard he was planning a revolt, and they rode into Lehi to capture Joel. When it came time for his army to stand up and fight, they proved they just couldn't do it." The old man wiped his eyes with his sleeve. "They rode into town— there must have been at least fifty soldiers. They dragged Joel into the street and . . ." He sniffed loudly. "No one even tried to stop them. They all cowered away like rats in the light."

"He's dead?" Samson whispered in disbelief.

"Yes, I'm afraid so," the old man replied gravely.

"What about Hannah?"

Simeon just shook his head sadly. "The only consolation is that she was not taken prisoner. They killed her quickly."

Samson clenched his fists and fought down the urge to throw something. He felt a rage boil in the pit of his stomach that burned like acid. He stood up and raked his hands through his hair. He paced back and forth in the small house like a caged animal.

"The children are alive," the old man said, trying to sound hopeful. "Joel and Hannah had another daughter three years ago. Both girls are living with my daughter and her new husband. They are very loved and well cared for."

Samson felt as though he was suffocating. "How could this happen? The priest in Shiloh said he saw them and they were safe. Alvah said the Philistines had stopped looking for them." His breathing became quick and shallow, and he started to feel light-headed.

"Sit down, Samson. I know this is upsetting, but you have to calm down. There's nothing we can do . . ."

"Really?" Samson almost shouted. "Is there really nothing we can do? Don't you think we've been doing nothing long enough?" His voice grew louder and stronger with every word.

"Samson, sit—"

"No! I can't sit by and watch this anymore! I have to do something! *We* have to do something! We can't allow those Philistines to take what they want and kill whoever gets in their way. God doesn't want this for His people!"

"But what are you going to do? You're only one man."

"Yes, and maybe I'll have to do it alone. If no one else will stand up, I will!"

"Where do you even start?" Simeon asked helplessly.

"I'll go back to where it all started—Timnah. I'll pay a visit to my cousin, Alvah. I'm surprised he didn't mention that Joel had been killed. He must have known. He lied to me just like those Philistines in Ashkelon. They're liars and criminals and murderers!" His voice seemed to shake the mud-brick walls of the house.

Samson ranted and paced for several more minutes until he finally sat down, feeling unexplainably exhausted.

"Stay here tonight," the old man said softly, pushing a cup of water toward Samson. "Tomorrow, I will send you to Timnah with all the supplies you will need and all the prayers I can give. I wish I could do more."

CHAPTER 32

Samson left early the next morning and headed west again. He passed through the familiar lands that he had grown up on and saw his father's house on the hillside. He desperately wanted to go home to see his family, but the thought of having to tell them what had happened to Joel and Hannah made him keep walking.

He camped that evening in a familiar cave that he had used in years past when he took the flocks to pasture in the area. As he sat alone by the mouth of the cave staring at his fire, the rage that had been driving him all day finally cooled and became a dull ache. He wanted to cry, but no tears would come. The priest in Shiloh had filled him with the hope of finding Joel, but he was too late. If only he had come sooner, he may have even been able to save Joel and maybe even help him keep his army together. The grief and regret seemed almost too much to bear. In his sorrow, the only One he could reach out to was Yahweh. Samson poured out his heart, hoping to feel some kind of encouragement or peace, but all he felt was a cold, hard anger in the pit of his soul. If only God would give him comfort. If only He could take away the growing rage that threatened to choke him. Why couldn't he just have relief?

He was too restless to sleep, so he left the cave and sat out in the cold darkness, filling his lungs with the night air. In the distance he could hear the sound of animals moving around. As his eyes adjusted to the blackness, he could make out the forms of several jackals gradually making their way closer to his cave. He knew from past experience that they were no threat to him. They were probably just curious. He welcomed the distraction the little animals brought. He watched as more and more jackals came out of their hiding places and crept closer to him. There were dozens of them, all moving together in a family pack. He envied the little community of creatures who seemed able to work together better than any people he had met.

Now completely distracted, he began to crawl toward the animals. When he moved, they all froze. He patiently waited until they felt comfortable; then he moved just a little closer. Eventually, he was close enough to leap out and grab one of the small dogs by its tail. The animal yelped and whipped its head around to bite him on the hand. Samson instantly released the jackal, and it ran away with the rest of the pack close behind.

He grabbed his bleeding hand and cursed under his breath.

He walked back through the darkness to his cave and lay down. Sleep would not come. Instead, he tossed and turned on the hard ground, trying to form a plan to avenge his cousin and stop the Philistines from more destruction. The rage and restlessness were almost too much to control. He couldn't even think clearly enough to formulate a logical plan. Just sleep and find Alvah. That's all he could come up with. He closed his eyes and willed himself to rest. A few hours later, he gave up. Sleep or no sleep, he had to be on his way. He ate some of the food Simeon had given him and began the hike back into Timnah.

Samson arrived at Alvah's home slightly after midday. He banged on the door, ready to attack his cousin as soon as he answered. Instead, he was greeted by Alvah's mother.

"Oh, hello, Samson. Alvah is at work, but come in and I'll fix you something to eat."

He absentmindedly rubbed his right hand where he had been bitten by the jackal the night before. "I don't want to come in. I want to find Alvah." He didn't want to get sidetracked again.

"Samson, you're hurt. Please come in, and I will dress that wound for you." She took his hand and inspected the bite. "You have to clean this, or it will become infected." She gently led him inside and offered him a place to sit. He reluctantly accepted.

"When will Alvah be back?" he asked through clenched teeth as the woman washed and wrapped the inflamed sore on his hand.

"In a few hours. You can rest here until he returns. You look very tired."

Her kindness drew some of the venom from Samson. He tried desperately to hold on to his anger until he could deal with Alvah, but his strength seemed to evaporate. Maybe a little rest would do him some good.

"All right, but just for a little while. Please wake me when Alvah comes home." He followed his aunt to a back room and lay down on a sleeping mat that was offered to him. He thought he would close his eyes only long enough to regain his strength, but he fell soundly asleep and didn't wake until he felt Alvah standing over him.

CHAPTER 33

"Hello again, cousin," Alvah said loudly, shaking Samson from his sleep. "What brings you back to Timnah? Are you ready to meet some girls?"

Samson rubbed his eyes and tried to clear his head enough to remember why he was in Alvah's house. It all came back to him in a rush, and he jumped to his feet and lunged toward his Philistine cousin. Alvah was able to move just out of Samson's reach.

"What's the matter with you, Samson? Are you having a nightmare or something? It's me, Alvah!"

"I know perfectly well who you are. You're a traitor and a murderer!" Samson lunged again, this time grabbing the front of Alvah's cloak. "Joel is dead!" he hissed as he shook the smaller man.

"I had no idea," Alvah stammered, trying to get away. "I thought he was still hiding out in the south. How was I supposed to know? I'm not involved with the military. I'm just an apprentice ironsmith."

Samson put his hands around Alvah's neck and began to squeeze. Just then Alvah's mother entered the room and gasped. "Samson, let him go!"

He instantly released his cousin. He couldn't kill a man in front of his own mother—especially after she had been so kind to him. Shaking with rage, Samson struggled to regain control of himself. "I'm supposed to believe you had no idea Joel was dead? I'm sure the Philistines talked about an army that was being raised in Judah. They must have bragged about killing their leader. How could you not have heard anything about it?"

"The soldiers that killed Joel may not have even been from Timnah. They stopped looking for the escaped prisoners years ago. Maybe the soldiers were from Gaza or Ashkelon. They would have been more concerned about an uprising in the south." Alvah rubbed his neck and gasped between words.

Samson sank back down on the mat. He felt as though he was the one who had been physically shaken. "You really didn't know?" he asked, feeling ashamed.

"I don't expect you to believe me, Samson, not after what I did, but I really didn't know. I hoped as much as you did that Joel was still alive. Now I feel as though I'm responsible for his death."

Samson buried his face in his hands as Alvah's words sank in. "Maybe it wasn't your fault," he finally muttered. "Maybe the Philistines who killed him didn't even know he was the same man who escaped from Timnah. They probably were just trying to suppress an uprising." He looked up at Alvah but saw only his bruised neck. "I'm sorry," he whispered. "I had no right to come into your home and attack you like that."

Alvah sank down next to him, and the two sat in silence for a few moments. Alvah's mother left and returned with drinks for both of them. Samson looked up at her pain-filled eyes. "Please forgive me," he managed to say.

She placed her hand softly on the top of his head. "Of course I forgive you, Samson. You're still part of my family." Without another word, she turned and walked away.

Samson stayed with Alvah and his mother that evening. He slept fitfully on a mat right next to the man who had been the enemy in his mind for so long. He wondered if they could ever really trust one another.

The next morning after breakfast, Alvah took Samson out to show him around Timnah. "A lot has changed in the past several years," he said as he led Samson through the streets. "The city fortifications are better, the market is bigger, even Dagon's temple is expanding."

At the mention of the temple, Samson remembered the Philistine priestess who helped him escape when he was a child. "Can you take me to the temple?" Samson asked, trying to sound casual.

Alvah smiled, thinking perhaps Samson's interests were in the god Dagon. "Of course! You won't believe how magnificent it is. They are adding a second story so more people can worship there. When it's finished it will look like the temple in Gaza. I've never been there, but someday I hope to go. I hear it's the most beautiful temple in the world."

Samson wasn't listening. He didn't care about the temple in Gaza. He didn't care about Dagon. All he wanted to do was find the Philistine woman who had been the standard for perfection in his mind since he was a child.

As they approached the temple, the streets grew more crowded and noisy. Samson noticed an obvious difference between the crowds here and the crowds at the tabernacle of the Lord in Shiloh. Here the feelings of reverence and respect were missing. The crowds jostled each other and talked noisily. Dagon's temple seemed more like a tourist attraction than a place of worship.

Alvah led Samson through the crowd and into the temple. Inside, construction was going on in almost every corner. Samson couldn't imagine hearing hammers and chisels in the holy place of the God of heaven, but here the sounds of workers and their crude conversations bounced off the walls and filled the temple. Samson was taller than most of the people in the crowd, so he had no trouble seeing over their heads. He easily spotted the priests and priestesses who were dressed in colorful flowing fabric, but he did not see the woman from his childhood visit.

Alvah seemed to sense that Samson was looking for someone. "Do you know someone here?" he asked.

"No . . . well, I met a woman here that night that I came . . ." Even though Alvah knew he had helped Joel escape, Samson still didn't want to admit it openly. "Anyway, she was older, but very beautiful. I would like to see her again if she's still here." Samson tried to act casual, but he wasn't fooling Alvah.

"The priests and priestesses don't always stay in one place," he explained. "She may have been sent north to Gath or south to Gaza." He saw the disappointment in Samson's face. "Forget her; she's probably an old woman by now. Besides, there are many beautiful women in this town. You didn't forget about the lovely Peles and her little sister did you?"

Samson didn't answer, but his expression must have given him away.

Alvah laughed and slapped Samson on the back. "Come on. Let's go home and try to make you look civilized, and then we'll go pay a visit to the vineyards just outside of town."

"I'm not cutting my hair, and remember, I don't eat grapes," Samson started to object.

"Relax. I'm not going to try to change you, just help you to fit in a little better. You don't want to scare poor Peles away before you even get a chance to talk to her, do you?"

CHAPTER 33

Samson blushed again and obediently followed Alvah back to his house.

After a little explaining, Alvah's mother untied the leather thongs that had been holding Samson's hair away from his face. She combed through the tangled mass while Samson sat at her feet wincing and complaining like a child with every pull. She divided his hair into seven sections, one in the back and three on each side, and then she braided them neatly and tied them in place. Though the Philistines generally kept their hair short, Alvah's mother had spent enough time living with the Israelites to know what was fashionable. While she combed and braided, her son left to ask his boss if he could have the day off. When he returned, he found his formerly wild Nazirite cousin looking much tamer. His mother had managed to subdue Samson's mass of hair, comb and clean his beard, and even find more stylish Philistine clothing for him to wear.

"You look so . . . different," Alvah stammered when he walked in the room. "Where's your ugly black goat-hair cloak?"

Samson fidgeted and pulled at the thin red material that now partially covered his body. "Your mother said you don't wear this one anymore. She had to take the sleeves off so I could move my arms, and it's probably way too short. I think I'll just wear my old one."

His aunt smiled and admired her handiwork. "No, you look so handsome, Samson. The ladies of Timnah won't be able to resist you now."

"But it's so tight," Samson complained as he wiggled in the lightweight fabric.

"It shows off your big, strong body," she replied as she tied a different girdle around his waist.

"Yeah," Alvah replied somewhat begrudgingly, "you look great—and speaking of ladies, we really should get going."

"I don't know, I feel kind of silly all dressed up. I'm not going to fit in with your friends. Maybe I should just—"

"Come on," Alvah interrupted. "It's going to be fun. It's about time I show you all Timnah has to offer."

Samson looked down at himself feeling insecure and uncertain. "Maybe I should just change my clothes and go back home."

Alvah sighed and shook his head. "All right then, I guess I'll just go visit Peles by myself. She may be disappointed that you're not there, but she'll get over it."

"What do you mean? Why would she be disappointed if I'm not there?"

115

"I don't know, it's just a feeling I got when I saw the two of you in the market, but it's probably nothing."

"What, what feeling?" Samson asked too quickly.

"It's just that I've never seen Peles look interested in anyone before, but for some reason, she seemed to like you."

"She did?"

"Yes, and that's when you looked like a wild animal from the hills. I can't imagine what she would do if she saw you now." Alvah changed into a nicer robe and tightened his girdle. "Oh well, I'll just tell her you had to go home. Less competition for me, I guess." He started to walk out the door.

"Wait," Samson called. "Maybe I'll go with you for a little while."

Alvah smiled and put his arm around his cousin's shoulder. "You won't be sorry, Samson."

Samson hoped he was right.

CHAPTER 34

Alvah and Samson walked back through the town. The sun was setting, and the last of the vendors from the market had long since gone home. The streets were still crowded with Philistines milling around aimlessly. Samson felt as though people were staring at him, but he didn't know why. He felt self-conscious about his hair and clothes but tried not to let it show. A woman with a painted face reached out and touched the top of Samson's bare arm, causing him to freeze in place.

"So, where are you boys going tonight?" she asked provocatively. "Would you like some company?"

Samson was about to talk to her, but Alvah pulled him away. "No, not her, Samson." He laughed as they walked on. "You sure have a weakness for the ladies, don't you?"

Samson didn't know what he meant, but he obediently followed.

The crowds thinned out as they reached the edge of town. In the distance, they could see farmhouses and fields dotting the slope into the Sorek Valley.

"See, Samson, it's not much different than Mahaneh-dan, is it? You may even find the people nicer here." Alvah quickened his pace as the two walked downhill toward a lighted house in the distance. When they arrived, Samson saw the house was large and well kept. There seemed to be a large plot of land in the distance, but the darkened sky made it difficult to see much more. Alvah led Samson to the courtyard where they found a handful of people eating and talking. An older man stood when he saw them approach.

"Hello, Phicol," Alvah greeted the man warmly. "I want you to meet my friend, Samson."

"Hello. Welcome to my home, Samson. Please, come and sit with us.

Some of your friends are here, Alvah. I think you know everyone."

Samson was led to a cushion and given a glass of wine, which he took but did not drink. He was introduced to the six other young men who were visiting with Phicol and his family. They had strange names, and Samson had trouble remembering them. He did not have trouble remembering Peles though. She was even more beautiful than he remembered from the market. She dutifully served her father and his guests but did not speak to anyone. All of the young men in the party talked politely to Phicol, but it was obvious to Samson that they were really there to see her.

At one point, she noticed Samson was not drinking his wine.

"Don't you like it?" she asked softly.

"Oh, I'm sure it's fine," he stammered. "It's just that I don't drink wine. I took a vow as a child . . ." He felt foolish and stopped talking.

"Let me get you something else," she offered kindly. He handed his cup to her, and their fingers touched for just a brief moment. It was enough to send a spark of heat through Samson's entire body.

He was glad she left quickly to refill the cup because he needed the time to compose himself. Alvah seemed to notice something was going on. "Are you all right, Samson? You're awfully quiet. How were the crops in the hills this year? Were they as plentiful as in the valley?" He tried to draw Samson into the conversation the men were having. Samson mumbled something about sheep and tried to look as though he was interested in grapes and wine, but his mind was spinning with thoughts of Peles.

When she returned, she handed Samson his cup. This time it was filled with sweet goat's milk. It was Samson's favorite. He smiled appreciatively at the girl, but was unable to say anything.

Throughout the evening, the two exchanged glances. Samson was oblivious to the young men, who were growing more and more impatient with his lack of participation in their conversation. One even spoke harshly to him, snapping him out of his Peles-induced daze.

"Are we boring you, Samson?" he asked

"No, no," Alvah quickly answered for him. "I think Samson's attention is just on something—or should I say someone—else." He laughed and the others joined in.

"I'm sorry," Samson stammered, feeling the color rise to his face. "What were you saying about the rainy season?"

Peles's father smiled warmly. "It's all right, Samson. Many young men are speechless the first time they come to my home. My daughters can be very distracting."

All the men chuckled, but Samson sensed some of them did not like having a new competitor.

"We should probably get home. Samson has been traveling, and I'm sure he's very tired." They both rose to leave. "Thank you, Phicol. As always, it was very nice to see you. I should have your plow blade finished tomorrow. Perhaps if Samson is still in town, I'll have him bring it to you."

Samson mumbled his thanks but found it difficult to take his eyes off the beautiful Philistine girl. As they walked through the darkness back into town, Samson was silent, but Alvah seemed to be able to read his thoughts.

"You really like her, don't you?" he asked quietly.

"I've never met anyone like her in my life. She's kind and beautiful and . . . well, she's exactly the kind of girl I would like to marry someday."

"Why 'someday'? She's single; you're single. Why don't you talk to her father about it?"

"Well, it looks like there are plenty of other men already interested," Samson began hesitantly.

"Yes, but Phicol loves his daughters, and he wants them to be happy. I didn't see Peles looking at anyone but you tonight. In fact, now that I think about it, I don't ever remember seeing her look at anyone like that before." Samson missed the slight edge of jealousy in his cousin's voice.

"Do you really think she likes me?" he asked hopefully.

"I don't know, but maybe you could find out tomorrow. You probably weren't paying attention, but I volunteered to have you deliver Phicol's plow blade that I've been repairing. It should be ready in the morning, and you will have a perfect excuse to go back to their house."

"Really?" Samson was ecstatic. "You know, Alvah, I really was wrong about you. I'm sorry I didn't trust you. You're turning out to be the best friend I've ever had!"

CHAPTER 35

Samson rose before dawn the next morning and waited impatiently for Alvah to wake up and go to work. He hovered outside the iron-smith shop while Alvah polished the plow blade for Phicol. When it was finished, Samson practically ran all the way down to the valley. When he arrived at Phicol's house, he found the younger daughter, Metsor, cleaning up the dishes from breakfast. She smiled and greeted Samson warmly.

"Are you here to see Peles?" she asked as though she knew a secret.

"Uh, no, actually I'm here to give your father his plow blade," he stammered. "But, is your sister here?" he added quickly.

She smiled and eyed him curiously. "Why do you look so wild?"

"Oh, you mean my hair and beard?"

"Yeah, that and well, everything. You just look so wild and different." She obviously wasn't as soft-spoken as her older sister.

"I'm a Nazirite, which means I don't eat certain foods or cut my hair."

"Are you some kind of warrior? You look really strong."

He was embarrassed by her questions, but she didn't seem malicious. "I've had a little bit of military training, but not much. I'm actually a shepherd."

She giggled softly. "You don't look like any shepherd I've ever seen."

Just then her father joined them in the courtyard. "Hello, Samson. Do you have my plow blade?"

"Yes, sir. Here it is." He held it out to the man. "I, uh, was wonder-ing, well, could I maybe talk to you for a moment?" He wished the younger sister was not watching him so intently.

"Sure, son. Let's go for a walk. I'll show you my vineyards." The two walked into the fields of recently harvested grapevines. As they walked, Samson struggled with what he wanted to say.

"Sir, I, uh . . ."

"You're interested in my daughter Peles," the man stated simply.

"Yes." Samson was relieved that he didn't have to come up with an eloquent way of stating the obvious.

Phicol laughed. "I could tell last night that something was cooking between the two of you. She asked me this morning if you were going to come over today. I have men visiting me all the time, and she never shows a bit of interest, but all of a sudden, she wants to know about the wild long-haired man from the hills." He patted Samson on the back. "Unfortunately, son, we may have just one little problem."

Samson's heart fell. "What?"

"You're an Israelite, and we're Philistines. Now, I know for us it isn't a problem, but I don't imagine your parents will be pleased. I understand it is frowned upon in your culture to marry people who don't worship your god."

"Oh, that's no problem," Samson replied without thinking. "My parents want me to get married. They'll love her as much as I do. I just know they will." Once Samson started talking he seemed unable to stop. "My father and I can build an addition onto his house, and she can live there with my family. It isn't far, so you can come see her whenever you want. And, of course, I'll bring her here whenever she wants to see you."

"Easy now, Samson. Let's take one thing at a time. Before you start any building projects, I think maybe we should sit down with your parents and talk about all of this. Do you think they would be willing to come here to meet us?"

"I can get them to come," Samson said confidently. "Once they meet you and see how perfect your daughter is, I'm sure they won't have any objections to my marrying her. I'll go home today to get them. May we come back tomorrow?"

"Slow down, son." Phicol chuckled and shook his head. "Peles isn't going to run off and marry someone else as soon as you turn your back. Just talk to your parents and invite them to visit us. I'll have my wife prepare a meal for them and we'll talk."

Samson nodded in agreement. He walked back to the house with Phicol, feeling as though his feet were not even touching the ground. As he was about to go back into town to tell Alvah the news, he saw Peles in the distance. He held his hand up to her in greeting. Even from a distance, Samson could see the smile light up her beautiful face. He turned and ran all the way back to Timnah.

Chapter 36

Samson went straight to the ironsmith shop, where he found Alvah pounding a long sword into shape. He quickly told him about the conversation he had with Phicol. It was decided that he would go straight back to Zorah to tell his parents about his desire to marry Peles.

It wasn't until Samson was almost to his father's house that a shadow of doubt darkened his mood. What if his parents didn't approve of his marrying a Philistine? What if Peles was treated like an outsider the way Alvah and his mother had been treated for years?

He quickly shrugged it off. He didn't care what anyone thought. He loved her. He wanted to marry her. His parents would just have to understand that she was going to be part of their family.

When he arrived home, his mother was busy preparing the evening meal, and his father was off in the fields with his brothers. When Sarai saw him coming, she ran to greet him.

"Oh, Samson, you're home. I missed you so much. You look different. Where did you get these clothes? There are no tassels on this robe. How will anyone know you're an Israelite? What have you done with your hair?" She kissed him on both cheeks. "Oh never mind; you're home." She led him inside and gave him some milk. "Did you find Joel? Is he safe?" she asked as she bustled around trying to make her son comfortable.

Samson felt a wave of guilt wash over him. Somehow he had forgotten all about Joel and Hannah while he was in Timnah.

"No, Mother, they are both dead," he said simply.

She gasped and bit her lip. "The Philistines found him?"

"I don't think they knew he was the same man who had escaped. He was raising an army in Judah, so the Philistines made an example of him."

123

Tears slid down her wrinkled cheeks, and she sat down next to him. "Your uncle Asahel will be heartbroken." She was quiet for a moment. "Well, at least we all know. Sometimes it's harder to be left wondering." She patted his hand, and the two sat in silence for a while.

"When will Father be home?" he finally asked. "I have some news for you both, but I want to wait until you're together."

She smiled and tried to read his face for clues to his secret. "He'll be home for dinner. He and the boys took the sheep to the northern pastures. They should be home soon. Why don't you unpack while you wait?" She looked around for his pack. "Where are your things?"

"They're gone," he said. "Everything was stolen from me while I was in Ashkelon. I ran into a gang of Philistine soldiers' sons, who turned out to be nothing more than common thieves."

"Your sword . . ." she began.

"Yes, they took it along with my clothes and the money Father gave me."

"Did they take what you were wearing? Is that why you have on these strange Philistine clothes?"

Samson had forgotten about Alvah's robe. He figured that he probably should have changed back into his old clothes before coming home, but his mind was too filled with thoughts of Peles to think about practical things.

"No, I got this in Timnah. I know it's different, but I kind of like it." He spun around, showing his mother his new look.

"Timnah? What were you doing there?" she asked looking concerned.

"I was just trying to get information about Joel."

"Well, I'm not sure I like the new cloak. It doesn't even cover your arms. Winter is coming, and it's going to get cold. I'll start making you something new right away."

"These clothes are fine, Mother. You don't have to make anything else."

"Nonsense. I just wish I had something for you to wear now. Nothing your father has will fit you; you're much too big. But it won't take me long to make something."

The conversation was interrupted by the sound of Samson's brothers in the distance. He opened the door and ran outside to watch the twins herding the sheep back into their enclosure. The youngest brother, Aaron, led their father by the arm. Samson wondered why his father still went out with the sheep when his sons were perfectly capable of doing it without him.

When Elihu saw Samson in the doorway, he ran to him and greeted him with a hug. Hosah was close behind him.

"Welcome home, Samson! How was your trip?" Hosah asked.

"Well, I have a lot to tell all of you. Come on inside and I'll fill you in," Samson answered, feeling a mixture of joy and dread at the thought of making his big announcement.

CHAPTER 37

Samson didn't get the reaction from his parents he was hoping for when he told them he planned to marry a Philistine girl. His mother cried and his father paced the floor. All three of his brothers sat in stunned silence.

"Can't you find a girl from any of our own people?" His father was practically yelling. "Someone from my brother's family, someone from Shiloh—you couldn't find one girl in the entire country that isn't a Philistine!"

"But Peles is beautiful and sweet. Father, I love her!"

"But she's a Philistine, and you're an Israelite," Manoah continued. "Not only an Israelite either—you are also a Nazirite. You're the one who is supposed to deliver us from the Philistines. You're not supposed to marry one!"

Samson stood up, almost knocking over the table. "I love her and I will marry her!" he shouted. His father looked stunned and hurt. "You wanted me to find a wife, and I've found someone I want to marry. No, she's not the stuck-up daughter of your nephew; she's not a plain, judgmental Israelite. She's a Philistine, and she's kinder to me than any other girl has ever been. She doesn't care that I don't drink wine; she doesn't care that I look different. In fact, I think she may even like me. I want her! I want you and Mother to go to Timnah and get her for me!" His voice became higher and higher as he spoke, making him sound more like a child.

His father took a long, shaky breath. "You really have your mind set on this, don't you?" he finally asked.

"Yes."

"Very well, we'll go to Timnah tomorrow to meet this girl and her

126

family. I'll prepare the necessary gifts for her father."

Samson didn't care that both of his parents looked older and more careworn than they had ever looked before. He didn't care that he was crushing their dreams for his future. All he cared about was seeing Peles again and asking her to be his wife. *Once we are married, everything else will work out,* he rationalized.

"I'll leave at dawn to tell her parents you're coming. I'm sure her father will want to prepare a feast for you." Samson spoke excitedly. "You all can come whenever you're ready. Just plan to be there by dinner. Should I take a lamb for her father?" He didn't wait for his parents to respond. "Yes, I'll pick one in the morning. I'm sure her mother will have time to prepare it before you get there. It's not that they couldn't provide their own lamb; I just don't want to go back empty-handed. They have plenty of money. You should see their house and all the land they own. I just think it would be nice if we provide something for the feast, don't you? You can take whatever else you would like to give for a bride price, but I'm going to pick a really fat lamb to take for dinner. You'll love her father; he's a very nice man, and Mother, you won't believe how beautiful she is . . ." Samson rambled on and on while his family sat in silence. At last his mother rose to go to bed.

"I'm glad you're happy, son," she spoke softly. "I hope the Lord will find a way to work all of this out."

"I am happy, Mother. I've never been so happy in my life." He stood to face her, and he held both of her hands in his. "You'll see; everything will be just fine. We'll build an addition on the house and live here with you. You'll learn to love her just as much as I do. You'll see."

"It would be nice to have you settled and content," she said sincerely.

Manoah made a noise in his throat and quickly excused himself from the room.

"Father, it will be all right," he called after Manoah. "Everything is going to fall into place now. I just know it."

CHAPTER 38

Samson's dreams were filled with images of Peles's face, her smile, and her small, delicate, hands. He woke feeling ready to take on anything. After washing and eating a quick breakfast, he went to the animal enclosure and picked the best lamb from his father's flock. He then drove the ewe down the hillside toward Timnah. The sun was not completely up as Samson walked through the familiar valley. The lamb wandered ahead, nibbling as she walked. Then out of the corner of his eye, Samson thought he saw something moving in a field of tall grass. He stopped to look, but whatever it was had disappeared. The lamb began bleating pitifully, so he quickly caught up to her to see what was wrong. She stood unmoving and terrified.

"What is it?" Samson whispered to the little sheep. "What are you afraid of?"

Silence was his only answer.

"Come on," he said to the lamb as he slowly began to walk forward, keeping his eyes and ears alert to anything that might be lurking in the tall grass. Again the lamb bleated, refusing to move any farther.

He knew the sheep, especially the young ones, were often afraid of just about everything. Sometimes they wouldn't even cross their own shadows; but for some reason, he felt the lamb might sense real danger this time. He heard a soft crunching sound as something nearby took a step closer. The thin hairs on his neck stood on end, and he suddenly felt as frightened as the helpless lamb.

"Who's out there?" he called toward the grass.

He sensed that whatever was in the grass was very close now.

"Show yourself," he called, sounding more confident than he felt. Maybe it was robbers. Maybe it was just a jackal. He had no way of knowing unless he faced it.

CHAPTER 38

The lamb still stood as if frozen. Samson noticed his own breath was fast and shallow. He took a deep breath and tried to steady his nerves.

He heard another soft step moving toward him. He spun around to make sure there was nothing behind him, but then he realized that the predator could come from any direction. He turned again, feeling trapped and frightened.

Just then, a huge golden-colored beast leapt out of the grass and landed in front of him. It was a young male lion whose mane was not yet fully grown. The giant animal shook its hairy head and growled. Samson had been warned there were lions in the area, but he had never seen one before. He had even suspected that they were just legends to keep shepherds alert. But here he was, face-to-face with a killer that was almost twice his weight and at least as tall if it stood on its back paws.

The lamb bleated again, but the lion never took his eyes off of Samson. It seemed strange that the animal would not go after the easier target. The two stared at each other. Samson felt paralyzed by fear. *Lord, help me,* he silently prayed. *I can't die now; I have too many plans, too many hopes for the future. Please, give me strength.*

At that moment, the lion sprang toward him. While it was still mid-lunge, Samson reached up and grabbed the beast's front legs. Without any planning, he spread his arms as wide as he could, and to his amazement, the lion started to rip in half. It let out a roar as Samson continued to tear the animal apart as if it were as small and frail as a year-old goat that was being sacrificed to God. He released the front paws, and the huge beast landed with a thud at his feet. He stared in shock at the two pieces of the dead lion. He looked down at his hands that were now shaking violently. There wasn't a drop of blood on them. The lamb *baaed* again, snapping him back to reality. His stomach rolled and he dropped to his knees, vomiting into the tall grass. He knelt there for quite a while, trying to calm himself. Whenever he looked over his shoulder at the mound of golden fur, he felt sick again. Eventually, his stomach was empty and his heart stopped pounding. He stood up and tried to compose himself. It seemed like a dream, but there was the dead lion right in front of him. He checked himself for injuries, but there were none. He had somehow killed the giant beast without any kind of weapon, and he didn't even have a scratch on him. It was impossible! He had never even heard stories as a child about anyone strong enough to kill a lion with his bare hands. But here he stood, the proof of his strength and might in a pile at his feet. His silent prayer and its immediate answer were completely forgotten.

He suddenly remembered Peles and his mission. He also remembered that his family would be taking this same path to Timnah. He didn't want them to see what he had done to the lion. It would only frighten them. He grabbed the back legs of the animal and dragged it into the grass, first looking around to make sure no one had seen him. Still shaking, he picked up the lamb, put her over his shoulders, and quickened his pace.

When he arrived at Peles's vineyard, he was winded and shaken. He set the sheep down and walked through the rows of grapevines trying to calm himself. He wasn't paying attention to where he was going, and he almost walked right into Peles, who was returning from the winepress.

"Oh, Samson," she said, obviously startled. "I didn't know you were here. Does my father know?"

"No, I just got here. I haven't seen anyone yet." He instantly felt better when he saw her.

"Well, let me take you to the house." She saw the little lamb for the first time. "Did you bring that?" she asked.

"Yes, it's for you." He picked the animal up and placed it back on his shoulders. "My family is coming this afternoon to meet your family, and I thought maybe we could have dinner together."

"They're coming to meet me?" she asked smiling. "Why?"

"I, uh, I told them about you, and they wanted to meet you." He suddenly felt shy. "I was hoping maybe you might agree to, well . . . I was wondering if you would marry me." His words came out in a rush at the end.

Her face lit up, and Samson thought she was even more beautiful than before. "I would love to marry you, Samson!" she exclaimed. She took his hand, and they ran together to her father's house.

"Mother, Father, Metsor!" she called as they approached the courtyard. "Come quick. Samson is here, and he's asked me to marry him!"

Her family greeted Samson warmly, and everyone seemed happy with the news—much happier than his own family had been. He told them his parents were on the way, and he gave them the lamb to prepare for dinner. Peles left with her mother and younger sister to prepare the feast while Samson discussed plans with Phicol. The two men seemed to have a natural, easy connection. It didn't seem to matter to Phicol that Samson was different. The older man embraced him as a son and welcomed him with open arms. Samson hoped his parents would be as accepting.

CHAPTER 39

Samson's mother and father arrived late that afternoon. They tried to be friendly, but their eyes were sad above the plastered-on smiles. Peles's parents were just as warm and welcoming as they had been to Samson. Phicol gave the best of his wine and food, and before long, everyone started to relax.

Throughout the evening, Samson and Peles couldn't keep their eyes off each other. She served him attentively and took every opportunity she could to make him comfortable. He ate and drank far more than he would have otherwise just so she would have to come close to him. Every time their fingertips brushed, he felt his face turn red. He couldn't wait until she was his wife. He dreamed of taking her to his home in the hills. He wanted to show her all the fields and paths around Zorah that he knew and loved so much. All of his insecurities about not fitting in and his worries about how God wanted him to free his people were forgotten. All he could think about was having Peles for his wife. But first, their fathers had to work out the details.

By the end of the evening, arrangements had been made for a wedding to take place as soon as an addition could be added to Manoah's house. The parents all agreed that there was no rush, which was obviously disappointing to Samson.

Phicol invited the family to spend the night, an offer that Manoah initially resisted. Samson didn't seem to notice how difficult it was for his family to put aside all of the feelings they had about Philistines just to make him happy. They had never before stepped inside a Philistine home, not to mention eaten with a Philistine family or slept in their house. But Phicol finally convinced them that it would be dangerous to travel back home in the dark, so they stayed. Samson was placed on a sleeping mat between his father and Phicol, while Peles slept in a separate room between their mothers. He wondered if she had as much trouble sleeping as he did.

The next morning, Samson and his family left, promising to return in a few months. The trip home was quiet. Manoah and Sarai walked in grim silence. Samson could think of nothing but Peles and the plans for their new home. When they arrived in Zorah, Samson immediately began building the addition that he and his wife would share. He worked almost without rest until the rains came and forced him indoors. For nearly two full months the rain fell, making it impossible for him to do anything other than brood in the house. He nearly drove his family crazy during those long weeks. Finally, the sun came out, and Samson was ready to resume construction. As soon as most of the work was finished on the apartment, he informed his parents that he was going back to Timnah. He wanted to tell Peles's family that they could start inviting the wedding guests and making the necessary preparations.

When he arrived at Phicol's house, he was surprised to find his cousin Alvah there.

"Well, here comes our bridegroom!" Alvah called warmly when he saw Samson approaching. They slapped each other on their backs and sat down together with Phicol.

"I'm almost ready to bring Peles home," Samson informed the men. "The house is ready enough for us to live in."

"Well then, I guess we should start the wedding plans!" Phicol said merrily. "You'll need guests and attendants. Will your relatives and friends be coming?"

Samson looked down at his sandaled feet. "No, just my father. My mother and brothers will stay home, but they will send anything you need."

"What about the rest of your family? Don't you have grandparents or aunts and uncles that would like to come?"

"It's too far for them to travel," Alvah quickly interjected. "Don't worry about any of that, Samson. I'll take care of finding groomsmen for you."

Samson gave him a grateful smile. "I'd like you to be my best man if you're willing. You've been a good friend to me; besides, we *are* cousins."

"You two are related?" Phicol asked in shock. "Alvah, I didn't know you were an Israelite. I thought you were one of us." Samson was a little surprised at Phicol's reaction. He had never known him to have any prejudices.

"Well, uh, not really," Alvah stammered. "My father was an Israelite, but I have a Philistine mother and a Philistine god, so I'm not really an Israelite."

"I see, I see," Phicol said, returning to his normal easy manner. "It doesn't really matter, does it? We're all going to be family soon enough. Samson, won't you stay and have dinner with us?"

Samson wasn't sure why, but he suddenly wanted to leave. That old familiar feeling of being an outsider was coming back to haunt him.

"No, thank you. I should get back before dark."

"But don't you want to see Peles before you leave?"

"No, I really should be going. I'll see her soon enough." He surprised even himself with his answer.

As he made his way back through the Sorek Valley, he heard a buzzing sound just off the path. He could see a few bees flying overhead, and he wondered what they were doing there. He pushed aside the tall grass and was surprised to find the decomposing body of the lion he had killed months before. The bees had made a nest inside the carcass. He knelt down next to the lion and saw there was honey inside. He knew he wasn't supposed to touch the dead body—it was part of his Nazirite vow. And eating something out of an unclean animal was off limits, too, but he didn't care. He wanted to taste the fresh honey. The fact that he shouldn't touch it made him want it even more. He carefully put his hand inside the lion and scooped out a handful of the golden liquid. He tasted it and it was delicious. He wanted to take some home to his parents, but he didn't have anything to carry it in. After a little searching he found a large branch that had fallen from an acacia tree during the winter storms. Using the dagger strapped to his thigh, he carved a makeshift bowl and filled it with the honey. He felt very pleased with himself, and his doubts about Peles and her family were soon forgotten—at least for the moment.

CHAPTER 40

When Samson reached home, he shared the honey with his family, but he didn't tell them where he had gotten it. He didn't want to explain about the lion, and he certainly didn't want his parents to know he had broken his Nazirite vow again. Once the sweet taste of the honey had worn off, he did feel a little ashamed of himself. It seemed the only part of the covenant he was able to successfully keep was not cutting his hair, and that really didn't require any kind of sacrifice on his part. Anyone could grow their hair long.

Talking about plans for the upcoming wedding helped Samson forget his feelings of guilt. His mother had been busy all winter making new clothes for him. She had already given him a new heavy black cloak that he had worn throughout the cold rainy months, but as his wedding day approached, she presented him with a new robe to wear for the weeklong feast. Samson was disappointed when he saw the coarse brown-and-black striped garment complete with the blue tassels that were sewn onto all the cloaks of Israelite males to remind them to keep God's law. He wanted to wear rich clothes like the Philistines. Because he didn't want to hurt her feelings, Samson accepted the gift and politely thanked her, but without enthusiasm. He was completely oblivious to the pained look in her eyes after he walked away.

The days before the wedding celebration was to begin, they packed the wooden cart with dried peas, lentils, melons, and cucumbers and gifts for Peles's family. They also recounted the sum of money that was agreed upon by the two fathers. The next day Manoah and Samson left for Timnah.

When they reached Phicol's home, thirty young men waited for them in the courtyard. They all shouted loudly and greeted Samson like a long-lost friend. He recognized a few of them from his first visit to Phicol's house, but the rest were complete strangers. Alvah, of course, was there, leading all of the festivities and helping to make everyone feel comfortable. When the sun started to set, Phicol produced torches for Samson and the groomsmen to carry. He then told Samson where to find his new bride. She had been hidden away in the house with the other women until it was time for the wedding. Samson led the men to the house and waited at the doorway, feeling as though his heart would burst in his chest. Finally, Peles arrived, looking more stunning than ever. Alvah and several of the other young men sucked in their breath when they saw her. She wore a lightweight purple robe with a red girdle tied at the waist. On her head she wore a garland of ten silver coins. Samson was glad that his mother wasn't there to see her unveiled hair and face. He knew she would have considered Peles to be immodest, but he thought she looked perfect. Phicol took his daughter's hand and placed it in Samson's and announced that they were now married. It felt strange not to have an elder there to pronounce a blessing on the couple. There were no vows or promises, no prayers to God. It didn't feel like a wedding. He brushed the thoughts aside and focused instead on the delicate hand he held in his. The heat from her palm made his pulse race. She smiled up at him, looking shy and sweet. He knew at that moment that there was nothing in the world he wouldn't do for his new wife.

CHAPTER 41

The festivities began immediately and went well into the night. Phicol's wine flowed freely, making the young men louder and more boisterous as the evening progressed. Peles made a special batch of goat's milk with honey for Samson, but she must have added something else to it, because he started to feel more relaxed and talkative too. Late in the night after most of the older guests had gone home, Samson sat with his thirty attendants, his wife, and a few of her friends. The young men were talking and laughing loudly, trying to outdo one another with stories of their own strength and bravery. Samson wasn't interested in their pointless conversation. He sat next to his wife, counting the minutes until he could be alone with her.

"So, Samson," one inebriated attendant got his attention. "Why didn't you give us all new clothes for being your special wedding guests? Isn't that an Israelite custom too?"

"What makes you think he can afford clothes for all of us? Just look what he's wearing," another guest laughed.

Samson felt his face flush. The more these so-called friends talked, the less he liked them. He couldn't wait for the weeklong celebration to end so he could leave this place. He took another sip of his sweetened goat's milk. The honey in it reminded him of the lion he had killed. He wished he could tell these annoying braggarts what he was capable of. He wanted to throw the rotting lion down at their feet and show them what he could do to them if they kept prodding him.

"You don't talk much, do you, Samson?" another man interjected. "You look strong enough, but you must be pretty stupid to just sit there letting your friends insult you like that."

Alvah jumped to his cousin's defense. "Samson's not stupid. He tells very clever riddles. Go ahead, tell them one." He nudged Samson with his elbow.

Samson thought for a moment then stood up so everyone was looking straight at him. "You all want wedding clothes?" he asked through clenched teeth. "I'll tell you what. If you can solve my riddle, I'll give each of you a set of clothes." The men chuckled and talked among themselves.

"Not made out of goat hair like yours, I hope," one man slurred loudly.

"No. Fine linen garments. Nicer even than the ones you're wearing now." He went on without thinking for a moment where he would get such clothes. "But if you can't solve my riddle by the end of the week, you will have to give me thirty sets of linen clothes."

The men all whispered and plotted. "OK, Samson. It looks like you have a deal." Alvah spoke for the group. "Go ahead, tell us your riddle."

Samson thought for a moment. He had been working on this riddle ever since he found the honey in the lion, and now he just had to find the perfect way to phrase it.

"All right, here it is." He spoke loudly for all to hear, "Out of the eater, something to eat; out of the strong, something sweet."

The men were silent. They scratched their heads and looked at one another hoping someone else had the answer.

Finally, a few attempted to offer answers, but they were all wrong.

"Well, obviously we've had too much to drink to be able to solve it tonight," one man spoke. "But we'll have your answer tomorrow."

"Good. Then I'll see you all tomorrow." Samson took Peles's hands and lifted her to her feet. "Now, if you'll excuse us, my wife and I are ready to retire."

Alvah stood up with the couple. "Why don't you go on ahead, Samson. Let Peles have a few moments with her sister and her friends. We'll bring her to you shortly."

Samson looked at Peles's encouraging smile and reluctantly agreed. He left the group of Philistines and went to the tent that had been set up for the new couple to use for the week.

Once inside, he took off his course cloak, lit a lamp, and sat on his sleeping mat waiting for his wife to join him. He suddenly felt nervous and unsure of himself. Would he be a good husband? What if they had children? What kind of father would he be? Would he be able to teach his family to believe in Yahweh the way his father had taught him?

The sound outside interrupted his thoughts. The noisy party with their torches lit escorted the bride as far as the entrance to the tent and then they walked away amid crude comments and laughter. Samson rose to meet Peles, who entered looking like something out of a dream.

She prepared herself for bed then lay down next to him on the mat. He had looked forward to this moment for so long but before he could even tell her how much he loved her, she started talking.

"That was some riddle, Samson," she said, taking him by surprise.

He ignored her and leaned over to kiss her.

She pulled away and continued her conversation. "I really think you stumped them. I don't think they'll ever guess the answer." She ran her fingers through her long light-brown hair letting it flow over Samson's arm and chest. "Now that I'm your wife, you really shouldn't keep anything from me—not even something as unimportant as the answer to your riddle."

"Why would I tell you?" he asked. "I haven't told anyone—not even my parents. Besides, what difference does it make? It's just a game."

"It's not just a game!" her voice was higher and tighter than Samson had heard it before. "How are you going to get thirty linen garments? Do you know how much that will cost?"

"But I thought you said they would never figure out the answer," he replied, feeling confused and frustrated. This wasn't at all how he planned the evening to go.

Peles turned to face him. "They won't guess it, my love." She spoke softly now. "But, you really should at least tell me. You shouldn't keep secrets from your wife."

"How do I know you won't tell them?" he asked, feeling his suspicions rise.

"Don't you love me?" she cried.

"Of course I love you. I love you more than anything."

"Well, then you should tell me the answer to your riddle."

As frustrated as he was, her pouting mouth made him melt. He reached out to touch her but she pulled away again.

"I'm tired, Samson." She lay down with her back to him. "We'll talk about this in the morning." And that was how their first night as husband and wife ended.

CHAPTER 42

When Samson awoke the next morning, Peles was already gone. After washing and dressing, he went to the courtyard, where he found her making breakfast with her mother and sister.

"Good morning," he said, smiling hopefully at his wife. She only scowled at him and continued her work.

"Can't you let your mother do that?" he asked. "We only have a little bit of time to spend together before the guests return." Her cold stare told him that he was the last person she wanted to spend time with.

"Ah, here's the happy couple!" Phicol interrupted as he and Manoah joined them around the outdoor stove. "Did you young people have fun last night?"

When no one answered, Phicol's smile quickly faded. Manoah studied his son carefully, trying to figure out what was wrong.

"Why don't we go for a walk?" Manoah said, taking Samson by the arm. "It will be so crowded and noisy once the festivities resume that I'm sure we won't have a moment to ourselves again all week."

The two walked through the vineyard, not saying a word until they were far away from the others.

"What happened?" Manoah finally asked.

"I did something very foolish," Samson replied, looking down at his feet. "I made a bet with the groomsmen that they could not solve a riddle."

"What was the wager?"

"Thirty linen garments," he replied, feeling sick. "But that's not the worst of it. I think they are trying to turn my wife against me. She was so insistent that I tell her the answer that I can't help but wonder . . ."

Manoah raked his hand through his hair and sighed deeply. "Well, maybe things will be better today. I hope everyone will just forget all about it and enjoy the rest of the celebration."

"I don't know, Father. I just don't trust them. Any of them."

"Good!" Manoah exclaimed without thinking. "I, uh, I mean, it's good to be cautious." He stopped walking and turned to face his much taller son. "Samson, just be strong. It's what you're best at."

Both men turned and walked back toward the house, Samson silently dreading the rest of the week and Manoah silently praying that God's will would prevail.

When they reached the courtyard, they ate in silence and waited awkwardly for the guests to return. Alvah was the first to arrive, and then the rest of the attendants trickled in, looking tired and stiff. By early afternoon, everyone was ready to resume the festivities. Phicol brought out wine and food and everyone relaxed a little, but the tension hanging over the young people couldn't be washed away—even with a river of wine.

The entire week dragged on like this for Samson. Each afternoon the young men would try in vain to solve his riddle and each night, Peles would cry and plead and yell at him until they both went to sleep, exhausted and angry. On the final night of the feast, Peles looked desperate. As soon as they were both alone in their tent, she clung to him and wept. It was the first time she had touched him all week.

"Samson, if you love me at all, you'll tell me the answer to your riddle. If you don't, I'll die!" she sobbed.

Something inside him finally broke. He held her like a child and stroked her hair. "I do love you, Peles. I don't want to hurt you like this." He released her and put on his sandals. "Get dressed. I want to show you something . . . and bring a jar."

She looked confused, but she did as he asked and followed him outside. He took one of the torches and walked with his wife into the blackness beyond her father's home. When they reached the place where he had killed the lion, he gave her the torch and pulled the decomposing animal out of the tall grass.

"What is that?" she gasped.

"It's a lion I killed. The bees have made a nest in it, and it's full of honey." He took the jar she had brought, filled it, and showed it to her.

She held the torch closer to examine the contents of the jar then she stuck her finger in it and tasted the honey. She then studied the lion. "It looks like it was torn into pieces," she said in amazement. "How did you do that?"

"I don't know. I just pulled it apart with my bare hands." He suddenly felt embarrassed. "Peles, you know I'm a Nazirite, but what you don't know is that God has given me amazing strength. There have been times in my life that I could do things that other men can't do."

She looked at him with an awe and respect that washed away any feelings of anger the two had been feeling during the week.

"Why are you showing me this?" she asked softly.

"This is my riddle. Out of the eater, something to eat; out of the strong, something sweet."

"Oh, Samson," she cried, kissing him all over his bearded face. "You do love me! I'm sorry I've been so awful to you. None of this riddle nonsense even matters. If you're strong enough to kill a lion, you can do anything."

Samson wasn't listening to anything she was saying. Her kisses seemed to wash away any reasoning abilities he had.

"Let's go home, husband." She took his hand and led him back to their tent, where Samson fell even more deeply in love with her.

CHAPTER 43

Samson slept late the next morning, and when he finally stepped out of his tent into the bright sunlight, he saw the guests were already arriving for the final day of the feast. When he found Peles working with her mother, he didn't get the greeting he expected. He had felt they had finally broken down the wall between them, but she seemed cold and distant again. The angry glare she had been giving him the previous mornings was replaced with something that looked like fear and regret. Samson knew he wouldn't be able to speak with her about it while her mother was there, so he decided to go greet his attendants, who seemed already to be celebrating.

"There he is!" one of them called when Samson approached.

Everyone smiled at him and slapped him on the back. He didn't understand why their attitudes toward him had changed so drastically. Alvah made a toast to him and his lovely wife Peles, and all the men drank to their health and fertility. Samson eventually let his guard down and sat with the men, joking and talking throughout the afternoon. He still felt uncomfortable with some of their conversation topics, but he knew it was the last day he would have to spend with them, so he tried to make the best of it. Peles was unexplainably distant all day. She kept herself busy serving food and drinks, which Samson thought was strange considering the other women had been doing it without her all week. He shrugged it off and assumed she just wanted to spend some time with her family before she left for Zorah with him the next morning.

As the sun descended in the sky, one of the attendants stood up to get everyone's attention. "As most of you know, our Hebrew host here has been having a little fun at our expense all week." He swayed slightly and took another drink from the cup that seemed to be giving him courage.

"A Philistine groom would never invite his guests over to steal from them, but we all know the Israelites aren't as well mannered."

Samson stood up and faced the man. "How dare you insult me in front of my guests?" he growled. "I haven't stolen a thing from you. My father and Peles's father have been nothing but generous to all of you."

"Now, that's not exactly true, is it?" he replied sarcastically. "You gave us a riddle and expected us to be too stupid to solve it. You hoped we would have to give you the clothes off our backs. Well, Samson, we've solved your little riddle—so you won't be getting anything from us!"

"Really? Tell me then, what's the answer?" he stood so close to the man he could feel his breath in his face.

"What is sweeter than honey? What is stronger than a lion?" he said triumphantly, holding up the jar of honey Samson had given his wife the night before.

All thirty of the groomsmen cheered and hurled insults at Samson, who felt he could easily kill the man in front of him. Alvah stood up and quickly pulled the man back to protect him.

"You would have never solved that riddle if you had not convinced my wife to tell you the answer." He stared intensely at Peles, willing her to look at him, but she kept her head down and her eyes averted.

"I should have known I couldn't trust any of you Philistine dogs!" Samson roared, silencing everyone in the crowd. Without another word, he turned and left the party and marched straight out of town.

At first he didn't know where he was going, he just had to get away, but then his steps became more deliberate. He headed south toward the Philistine town of Ashkelon. Something inside of him guided him and pushed him forward. He had no plan. He just knew he wanted to see the men who had stolen Joel's sword.

Even though it had been several months since his one and only visit, and it was now completely dark, Samson had no trouble finding the courtyard that Saph had invited him to. When he arrived, he saw the same crowd gathered that had taken him in as a friend only to steal everything he had.

He walked into the center of the crowd and stood towering over them. Slowly the music died, and all of the talking stopped. Everyone turned to stare at this tall man who looked strangely familiar.

"Hello, Saph," he said, spotting the man who had led him here on his last visit. "I've come for my sword."

"Oh, hello. Samson, is it?" the man asked stepping forward. "I'm not sure I know what sword you're talking about."

"You know perfectly well what I'm talking about." Samson grabbed the man by the front of his fine linen cloak. "You took the Philistine sword my cousin gave me, and I want it back."

Saph laughed in his face. "You know perfectly well that sword didn't belong to you. Why would a dirty Hebrew like you have a fine soldier's weapon like that anyway?"

Samson shook the man and felt an uncontrollable rage rise up in him.

"I don't have it!" the man shouted, sensing he was in real danger. "I sold it. It's long gone!"

Samson threw Saph across the courtyard as if he weighed nothing at all. The man landed with a thud and didn't get up. Saph's friends stood in shock for just a moment, but they quickly recovered and attacked Samson all at once. Samson grabbed the closest man and snapped his neck like a twig. The next man advanced, but he was thrown to the ground with such force, he landed in an impossibly twisted position. One after another, the men charged toward him, but he was able to predict their every move and easily deflect every attack they tried. The last few men standing realized that they were in trouble, so they ran. Samson was left alone standing in the middle of a heap of dead Philistines. He dropped to his knees, suddenly feeling as though he couldn't get enough air into his lungs. His hands started to shake, and for a moment, he thought he was going to be sick.

Eventually, his racing heart slowed, and he was able to think more clearly. He looked around at the young men scattered on the ground. Their brightly colored clothes were torn and bloody. That's when it came to him. He needed thirty sets of clothes to give to the men of Timnah. There had to be at least thirty men here. His Nazirite vow temporarily forgotten, he rummaged through the pile of bodies to find the largest man. He was pleased to see the man's clothes were not damaged and they were much nicer than the ones his mother had made for him, so he took them for himself. After discarding his heavy cloak and replacing it with the fine Philistine robe, he stripped the rest of the men of their belongings and tied them all into a bundle. He then began the long walk back to Peles's house.

He arrived just after sunrise and found drunken men sleeping around the courtyard. They must have had quite a celebration after he left.

"Wake up!" he shouted, as he threw the clothes onto the ground. The men stirred and rubbed their swollen eyes. "This is what you wanted—wedding clothes. Well, here they are!"

The men got up and looked through the clothes in disbelief. No one needed to ask how Samson got them, and no one felt brave enough to challenge him.

Manoah emerged from the house looking worried and haggard. Samson was relieved that he was safe. "Come on, Father." He walked to Manoah and gave him his arm. "We're going home."

CHAPTER 44

When Samson arrived home, he went straight to the addition he had built on his father's house and went to sleep. His mother went in periodically to check on him and to leave food and water, but he didn't wake up for almost two days. When he finally did open his eyes, he ate enough to feed an entire family, and then he went back to sleep. His parents were obviously worried about him, but no one questioned him. They realized he needed some time to work things out on his own. For almost two months, Samson wasn't much more than a shadow in his family's home. He did the work that was required of him. He ate the food that was set before him. Then he retired to his private quarters to sulk and pace and think. Sometimes he even prayed.

When it was time for the Passover, the family readied themselves to go to Mahaneh-dan. Samson didn't want to go, but his father convinced him that it would be good for him. Reluctantly, he agreed. When they reached Uncle Asahel's home, the family was greeted in the usual way; however, Samson noticed everyone was a little reserved around him. He was still included, but for some reason, he felt like more of an outsider than ever before.

After the family shared the unleavened bread and the lamb cooked with bitter herbs, they reclined on cushions around the fire to talk and visit. Passover was usually Samson's favorite holiday. No one drank fermented wine, so the mood was much less rowdy. He usually felt less different during this time of year, but not this time. The talk of the evening revolved around his cousin Martha, who was now happily married and expecting a child. Her sister, Deborah, was betrothed to marry a wealthy widower who lived in the neighboring town of Eshtaol. Deborah's father, Caleb, had been doing business with the man for years, and when his wife died in childbirth, leaving him with a newborn to care for, it was decided that Deborah would be his new wife. Caleb and the rest of the family seemed very pleased with the match. Samson wondered if Deborah was happy. Deep down, he hoped she was.

Samson just sat back and listened and watched. All the talk of marriage made him miss Peles. Since leaving Timnah, he had felt a series of emotions ranging from grief to anger, but mostly, he just hated his wife for betraying him. Watching Martha and her husband made him forget some of the anger he felt toward Peles. If only he could have her with him, away from the other Philistines, maybe everything would work out. He could teach her and her family about the true God of heaven. Maybe they would all leave their god, Dagon, behind and worship with him. The more he thought about it, the more certain he was he could change them.

As his family visited, he silently made plans. The harvest would begin soon, and it looked like it was going to be another bumper crop. He could bring Peles and her family to Mahaneh-dan for the feasts that followed the harvest. The Festival of Tabernacles was only a few months away. He could take them to Shiloh to worship and celebrate. He was sure God Himself could woo them away from Dagon. With his plans made, he started to relax and enjoy himself a little more.

When Samson and his family returned to Zorah after the Passover, he began making plans to go to Timnah. His was disappointed when his departure was delayed by various tasks that had to be completed. The weather was unusually hot and dry, so the herd had to be taken farther from home to find green pastures. Since his brothers were still quite young, he was given the task of tending the sheep until the later rains came to moisten the lands closer to home. He found good land south of his home in the area occupied by the tribe of Judah, so he set up camp in the now-familiar caves. Every evening, he watched the jackals come out to hunt. Through practice, he was now able to catch them without being bitten. During the days, he watched his animals closely. The dry weather made the predators more bold than usual. Samson occasionally found carcasses of animals that had probably been attacked by lions or bears. The lonely days passed, and Samson longed more and more to see his wife. His anger was now completely forgotten. Occasionally, he went to the town of Lehi to replenish his supplies. The old man he had rescued from Timnah still lived there with his family and Joel's two orphaned daughters. Samson was always received warmly and given whatever he needed. As the harvest time drew closer, he knew he should get back to Zorah so he could help his parents bring in the crops in their now expanding fields. The clouds over the hills looked heavy and dark, promising to bring the rain the fields needed to revive the withering crops. His experienced shepherd's eye knew the rain would also awaken the grass his herd needed to survive. He led the animals back home just before the rain came. He thanked Yahweh for providing exactly what he needed when he needed it.

Once his parents' field was harvested, there was nothing keeping Samson from going to Timnah to get his wife. He chose a young goat to give her father as a gift and led it down the familiar path to the Sorek Valley. When he drew near to the place where he had killed the lion, he left the path and went instead through the fields of wheat that were owned by the Philistines who had attended his wedding. He was afraid that seeing what was left of the lion would revive the anger he felt toward Peles.

The ground crunched under his feet as he made his way through the wheat fields. It was late afternoon, and the hot sun had been drying the mature plants all day. The valley didn't receive the same rain as the hills. Instead, the crops here were moistened each morning by mist coming in from the sea. As he looked at the full heads on the plants, he could see that the Philistines, too, were expecting a plentiful harvest.

He knew he was getting close to his wife's house when the wheat fields ended and the olive groves and vineyards began. Finally, Samson could see Phicol's house in the distance. Lights burned inside of the house, and he could almost picture Peles's beautiful face in the warm glow. When he got closer, he saw the place where the tent had been erected for his wedding week. In its place was a pile of discarded torches that had been used by the guests. He remembered the last night he had spent with Peles and the closeness he had felt toward her. He suddenly wanted to see her more than he wanted anything else in the world. He reached the front door and knocked. Phicol answered and seemed prepared to offer a smile and a warm greeting, but when he saw it was Samson, his face fell.

"Samson!" he exclaimed, obviously shocked. "What are you doing here?"

"Hello, Phicol. I've come to see my wife." Samson held the kid out to Phicol. "I brought this for you." He stood awkwardly in the growing darkness outside, waiting for an invitation to come in, but it never came.

"I, uh, Peles is not here," Phicol stammered.

"Well, where is she?"

"I thought you hated her. After you left, I uh . . ." Phicol looked nervous and embarrassed.

"What? What did you do, Phicol?" Samson felt his face flush.

"I gave her to your friend Alvah. He came for her right after you left. She's married to him now."

"How could you do that?" Samson yelled. "She was my wife! How could you just give her to someone else?"

"I never thought you would come back for her." Phicol's voice broke and he looked miserable. "You may have her younger sister, Metsor. People say she's even more beautiful than Peles."

Samson felt a rage boil up inside of him unlike anything he had ever felt before. "That's it!" he roared more to himself than to Phicol. "Now I have a right to get even with the Philistines. Now they'll see that they can't just take whatever they want from us!"

"Samson, I'm so sorry. I didn't know you would come back—Alvah said you were gone for good."

"Alvah!" Samson spat the word out of his mouth. "I should have known never to trust him. That's the last time I'll trust any of you! You will all pay for what you've done!" Samson stormed off, not knowing what to do next. When he saw the pile of torches, he had an idea. He scooped up as many torches as he could carry and headed to the fields. He knew there was no way he could raise an army of men to fight the Philistines, but he could easily raise another kind of army that could do a lot of damage. In a few hours, he caught three hundred jackals and tied them together by their tails. He then tied a lighted torch between them and turned them loose into the dry fields. The frightened animals ran in all directions, leaving a path of flames behind them. They burned all the wheat that was ready to be harvested as well as the vineyards and olive groves that would have yielded their fruits in a few months. By sunrise, the Philistines' crops had been completely devastated. But Samson's anger burned far more dangerously than the torches. He went home to prepare for the next battle.

CHAPTER 45

The next day, Samson returned to Timnah to find Alvah. From a distance, he could see the smoke still rising from the fields he had burned the night before. As he walked through town, he noticed the market was closed, and there were fewer people in the streets. Several Philistine soldiers eyed him suspiciously and whispered to each other as he passed by. Samson was too focused on his mission to notice that they were following him at a distance.

When he reached Alvah's house, he banged loudly on the door. When Alvah's mother answered, it was obvious she had been crying.

"What do you want?" she asked bitterly.

"I want Alvah."

"He's gone!" she cried.

"Where did he go?" Samson's anger was increasing.

"I don't know. They came before dawn this morning and took Peles. Alvah ran away so they wouldn't take him too."

Samson's head was swimming. "Who came? Where did they take Peles?"

"Alvah's friends. They took Peles back to her father's house and killed her. Because of what you did last night, they burned her and her family and everything they owned." Hatred flashed in her eyes as she spoke.

"And Alvah—where did he go?"

"I told you, he ran away! I don't know where he went. Maybe Ashkelon. Maybe Gaza. All I know is that Alvah is gone—and it's all your fault!"

Samson didn't have time to think. Someone had grabbed his arm. He whirled around and was confronted by several Philistine soldiers as well as some of the men who had attended him at his wedding. The man directly in front of him was the largest Philistine soldier he had ever seen. Before he could speak, the giant of a man punched him in the face. Samson's head jerked to the side. He tasted blood in his mouth but felt no pain. In the moment it took him to recover, he was able to calculate his attack. With clenched fists, he stood facing the soldier who hit him.

"That wasn't a good idea," Samson said as he spit blood at the huge sandaled feet of the Philistine.

"What are you going to do? There's only one of you and at least twenty of us," the soldier replied confidently.

Samson looked at the men who had attended him at his wedding. They were all wearing the clothes he had taken from the Ashkelon thieves.

"This will be the second time I've killed men wearing those robes," he threatened.

All of the attendants moved back, obviously intimidated.

"That's enough talking." The huge soldier grabbed the front of Samson's cloak. "Tie him up," he commanded his partner, who stood nearby with ropes in hand.

Every detail suddenly became clearer—the deep blue veins on the soldier's neck, the flare of his nostrils, the faint smell of smoke and sweat on the arm that held him. His heartbeat pounded loudly in his ears. The crowd around him disappeared, and he saw only the face of the man in front of him. With amazing speed, he lifted his left hand and brought it down on top of the soldier's arm, forcing him to release Samson's cloak. Before the man could react, Samson dropped his right arm back and sent a punch under the jaw of the soldier. He could feel the bone turn soft under his knuckles as his fist lifted the enormous man off the ground. The soldier's body flew through the air and thudded onto the ground. Immediately, another soldier stood before Samson. His soot-covered face was all Samson could see at that moment. He grabbed the man by the neck and flung him aside like an insect. Some of the Philistines who had attended his wedding tried to attack him in groups, but Samson easily shook them off, destroying anyone who came within arm's reach.

In what seemed like mere seconds, every one of the men had either fallen or run away. Samson was left standing alone with Alvah's mother in the door behind him. Her mouth was open in shock and horror.

"You're a monster," she whispered.

"I am what your people made me," he replied, without turning to face her. Then he left Timnah, swearing he would never return again.

151

He knew it was just a matter of time before the Philistines regrouped and came after him. If he went home, they would follow him and possibly hurt his family. So instead, he went south to the caves he had used many times in the past. He found a familiar cave in the Rock of Etam, and he lay down to try to rest. The walk had done little to calm him down, and he found it almost impossible to rest. He did finally fall asleep, but woke up a short time later feeling hungry and thirsty. It was now dark, so he thought it would be safe to go into the nearby town of Lehi to visit his friend Simeon. He knew the old man would give him something to eat. When he arrived, he could tell something was wrong. Simeon answered his knock, but he was obviously not happy to see him.

"Samson, you should not have come," the old man whispered, trying to keep the door closed as much as possible.

"Please let me in, Simeon. I'm so hungry and thirsty; I feel like I could die." Samson could hear angry voices coming from inside the house. "Who's in there, Simeon? Are you in trouble?" His own needs forgotten, he suddenly felt concern for the old man's safety.

"No, Samson, I'm not in trouble, but I'm afraid you might be."

"Who's here?" a deep voice called from inside. "Is it Samson?"

"How do they know about me?" Samson whispered. "Is it the Philistines?"

"No, it's the men of the village. They know you come to visit me, and they know what you did in Timnah. They're just afraid you'll bring trouble on them."

Samson pushed the door open and walked into the house, swelling with the now-familiar anger and frustration with his own people. "Why are you all here?" he asked, pushing past the frightened Simeon.

His sudden entrance silenced the Israelites. When the men saw Samson in person, their anger and fear was replaced with awe. One young man reached out and touched his hair. Another knelt in front of him.

He was momentarily shocked by their respect, but he quickly recovered. "If you're worried about a confrontation from the Philistines, you should be preparing for the attack. Why are you all sitting around here talking when you should be preparing for battle?"

Simeon brought him food and water and offered him a seat. Samson took it all gratefully.

"Samson, we think you did a great thing standing up to the Philistines like that, but we aren't prepared to do battle with them if they come looking for you," one well-dressed man spoke for the group.

"Why not?" Samson's voice boomed in the small house. "This would be a perfect time to attack. We can finally take the lands that are rightfully ours."

"But, Samson, there are so few of us and so many of them," another man interjected.

"That doesn't matter. God is ready to deliver us. All we have to do is allow Him to use us. Our strength is not in our numbers or in our skills; it's in our God!"

But the men were frightened and uncertain. Samson feared he would lose his barely controlled temper and take it out on his kinsmen. "I have to leave!" he exclaimed, feeling his anger rise. "When you're ready to fight, you can find me in the cave in the Rock of Etam." He took one more long drink of the water Simeon had given him and he rose to leave. His host smiled at him kindly, but the fear was still obvious in his eyes. Samson wondered if his people would ever stop being afraid.

CHAPTER 46

Samson hid out in the cave for two more days. He searched the area for food and water, but found none. He didn't dare go back to Simeon's house for fear of what might happen to his friend. On the third morning since his arrival, he was awakened by the sound of men outside his cave. At first, he thought the Philistines had found him, but then he recognized the voice calling him out of his cave. It was Simeon. *The men of Judah must have changed their minds about fighting. They are here to assemble an army!* Samson's heart leapt with joy at the thought of leading his people against the Philistines. When he stepped out into the growing morning sunlight, he was delighted to see thousands of his own people gathered outside. At last, he had his army. But then Simeon stepped forward, his head down and shoulders hunched.

"I'm sorry, my friend, but we've come to turn you over to the Philistines," he said miserably.

Samson's smile slowly faded. "What?" he asked in shock. "Why would you do that? We can fight them."

"I'm so sorry . . ." Simeon's voice trailed off. Samson thought he saw tears in the old man's eyes, but he couldn't manage to feel even a bit of sympathy for him. *I'm so tired of dealing with these cowards. How can they even call themselves men?*

A stranger wearing a fine robe with long tassels came forward and stood directly in front of Samson. His eyes shone with determination that barely concealed his fear. "Don't you know the Philistines are our rulers? They have an army ready to destroy us if we don't turn you over to them."

"Why have you done this to us?" another man spoke from the crowd.

"I did to them only what they did to me," Samson answered. "We can fight them!"

Simeon again stepped forward, holding ropes in his hands. "We've come to tie you up and hand you over to the Philistines."

"We can fight! There are enough of us here to do serious damage to the Philistines," Samson shouted to the crowd.

"We have no weapons or training. The Philistines are skilled warriors. We'll all be destroyed, and then they'll take our wives and children. We can't fight them."

Samson looked into the face of his friend, Simeon, standing in front of him. "Swear to me you won't kill me yourselves," he said softly.

"We won't kill you," Simeon promised.

"No, we'll just tie you up and hand you over to them. Maybe they'll spare us if we cooperate," another man said, taking the ropes from the reluctant old man.

Samson held his hands out and allowed his fellow Israelites to tie him up with the new ropes. Once secured, they led him back toward town. Before they reached the village, Samson heard shouting in the distance. The three thousand Israelites who had brought him this far now scattered when they saw the Philistines approaching. The metal of their helmets glinted in the sun, and the red feathers on top made the army look like a river of blood flowing toward him. Samson stood alone, bound with rope and looking completely vulnerable against the oncoming flood. He closed his eyes, took a deep breath, and whispered a prayer to God. When he opened his eyes, he felt an incredible power surging through him. Again he felt all of his senses heighten, and an intense strength seemed to take possession of his body. He snapped the ropes off of his wrists as though they had been singed by fire. He didn't have a weapon, not even the dagger he usually kept strapped to his thigh, so he quickly scanned the area for something to use against the oncoming army. The only thing he saw was the skeleton of a donkey that had probably been killed recently by a lion. He picked up the jawbone just as the first soldiers were nearing him. Their swords were drawn, swords identical to the one Joel had given him. They moved toward him in what seemed like slow motion. Samson heard nothing but his own heartbeat pounding in his ears. He swung the jawbone, hitting the first man across the side of the head. He hit him so hard, he knocked his helmet off, and the soldier fell dead in his tracks. Next, two men advanced simultaneously, but Samson swung the bone and hit them both. One after another, the soldiers charged, and Samson killed each one as he came within reach. He fought like this for hours as the sun climbed higher in the sky and the soldiers became fewer and fewer. When Samson had killed the last Philistine, he spun around, expecting to find another man ready to attack him, but all he found were bodies scattered on the ground. He gasped for air and felt his legs shake underneath him. The donkey jawbone slipped out of his hand and landed with a thud at his feet. He collapsed to his knees, in desperate need of water. Looking around for any Israelite men, he found no one. Samson tried to call out in case they were hiding in the caves, but he was too weak to do much more than whisper. Exhausted, he staggered from the battlefield toward the nearby town. He finally collapsed in a field, so dehydrated he felt as though he would die of thirst. "Oh, God!" he called out in a hoarse whisper. "You've given your servant this great victory, but now I'm going to die here of thirst." He lay his head down, feeling sure that he would never get up again, but then he heard a trickle nearby. He rose to his hands and knees and crawled toward the sound of the water. Right there in the dry dust, God had opened up a hollow place in the ground and made fresh cool water spring out. Samson drank deeply, feeling his strength return with every swallow.

Once revived, Samson walked back toward the cave he had been sleeping in so he could collect his belongings. All he wanted to do was leave this horrible place. To get back to the cave, he had to walk over the bodies of the men he had killed. There must have been a thousand of them. For the first time, it occurred to him that he had single-handedly killed all of them with nothing more than a donkey's jawbone. *Where are the three thousand men of Judah who came for me this morning? Didn't they realize they could have taken part in this victory? If I alone can defeat this many Philistines, what could I have done with three thousand men behind me? They are cowards—all of them.* Even his friend, Simeon, had come to hand him over to the enemy. He thought about Joel and how frustrating it must have been for him to try to lead these people. But that was Joel. Samson knew now without a doubt that he was different. He tried to count the number of men he had killed in Timnah, Ashkelon, and now here at the Rock of Etam. It had only been a few days, and he had done more to push back the Philistines by himself than anyone had done in generations. Samson was sure he could succeed where Joel had failed. Look what he had already accomplished. Nothing would stop him from defeating the rest of the Philistine army.

· PART 3 ·

CHAPTER 47

After his battle in Lehi, Samson became famous throughout the country. Israelites gathered around their fires at night, telling their children stories of the long-haired Nazirite who killed a thousand men with the jawbone of a donkey. The feared and hated Philistines instantly became the butt of many donkey jokes. But that ended when the soldiers burned a small village to the ground because the commander thought he heard a child braying like a donkey when his back was turned. That was all it took for the old familiar fear to settle back over the long-oppressed Israelites.

But Samson wasn't afraid. For several years, he traveled freely from town to town. He was always watched closely by the Philistine soldiers, but none of them could stop him. They came at him with every weapon and military tactic they had, but they soon learned that this man who was sent from the God of the Hebrews was indestructible. Occasionally a young, overzealous soldier would try to challenge him, but Samson put a quick end to that.

The Israelites throughout the country treated him like a hero when he came to their towns and villages. He was always given the best food and accommodations and encouraged to stay as long as possible. The Hebrews knew that if Samson was in their town, the Philistines wouldn't dare bother them. As the years passed, the people started calling him a judge. He was invited to sit at the gates of the cities to hear cases and settle disputes. At first he enjoyed the attention and respect, but he soon grew tired of listening to people drone on and on about their problems. He was a man of action in a world of complainers. His restlessness grew and filled him with a need to keep moving.

Though he longed for his home in Zorah, he spent little time there because he knew he was always being watched. If the Philistines found out where his family lived, they were sure to harm them in some way when Samson was not there to protect them. He avoided Mahaneh-dan for the same reason.

As Samson traveled, he tried to rally the Israelites to form an army, but he didn't have any success. In every town he visited, he found the men so subdued and frightened that they wouldn't even stand up to a single Philistine soldier, let alone an army of them. They all praised Samson for his strength and courage, but very few were willing to follow him. Eventually, he gave up his dream of leading his people into battle against the Philistines. It became clear to him that if he was going to defeat them, it would be alone.

Alone is the way that Samson felt much of the time. Though throngs of people came out to see him when he passed through town, and feasts were usually prepared in his honor, he felt as though no one really knew him or cared about him. He was respected by all but befriended by none. At times when he felt especially lonely, he thought about Peles. His anger and bitterness toward her were gone. All he remembered was that she had loved and accepted him—at least for one night.

The one place Samson finally found a friend was in Shiloh. He went there to celebrate the festivals as often as he could. It was the one place in the country that the Philistines did not follow him. They had seen enough of Samson's power to know that they didn't want to get too close to his God's dwelling place. In Shiloh, Samson was free to spend time with his family and catch up on everything that was happening back at home. It was there that he met the wives of his younger brothers and held their newborn babies. But it wasn't in the tents of his family that he felt the most comfortable; it was at the Tabernacle of the Lord. He went often to just watch the priests perform the daily sacrifices. People came from all over the country to offer thanks and praises to the God of heaven. It filled Samson with hope for his people. He had seen so much of the Philistine's influence on the Israelites that it made him happy to know there were still those who worshiped Yahweh fully and completely. This image of faithful believers is what gave him the strength to go on fighting for his people.

It was here at the tabernacle that Samson got to know the high priest and his family. He found out the man's name was Eli and that he had been serving as the high priest for only a few years before meeting Samson for the first time. Eli seemed to take an instant liking to Samson. When the crowds had gone home after Passover, he invited the younger man to come to his house for dinner. At home, Eli took off his jeweled ephod and high turban and was instantly transformed into a normal man. Samson watched him with his wife and two rambunctious sons and marveled at how ordinary they all seemed. The boys squabbled and argued, but Eli just tuned them out and went on visiting and enjoying his meal. After the family had gone to bed, Samson and Eli sat near the fire talking late into the night. They talked about the trials of their people, they talked about what could be done to stop the Philistines, and then they shared some of their deeper, more personal thoughts. Samson told Eli about the death of his cousin Joel and the loss of his wife Peles at the hands of the Philistines. Eli listened and offered comfort. By the end of the night, Samson felt more at peace than he had for years. He decided that he would make Shiloh his home for a while. He spent as much time as he could with Eli. The two men sat at the gates of the city together, hearing cases and discussing politics with those who were traveling through Shiloh. Day after day, Samson heard men telling of the horrible things the Philistines were doing throughout the country. Women and children were taken, men were killed, and entire towns were burned to the ground. There seemed to be nothing that could stop them. The people cried out to Samson and Eli and then went to the tabernacle to plead with God for deliverance. At first, Samson wept for the people, but then he became more apathetic. It was easy to forget how hard it was living under the Philistines' oppression when he was surrounded by the safety and comfort of Shiloh. Days slipped by, then years, and eventually, the cries for help from the demoralized travelers became nothing more than sad but distant stories. That all changed the day a messenger came from Zorah with news for Samson.

CHAPTER 48

Eli and Samson sat at the city gates one evening, waiting for the horn to blow for the evening sacrifices. Sometimes it surprised Samson that his friend didn't spend more of his free time at home with his wife and sons. The two boys obviously needed their father's guidance, but Eli seemed to prefer the quiet he found outside of his home. While the two men talked with a group of travelers from Lebonah, a young man approached them looking dirty and tired.

"Are you Samson, son of Manoah?" the man asked, trying to catch his breath.

"Yes. Who are you?"

"I'm a messenger sent from your brothers in Zorah."

"Get this man something to drink," Samson ordered a servant boy standing nearby. "Come and sit down."

The messenger gratefully accepted both the drink and the cushion that was offered to him.

"What is the message you have for me?" Samson asked, feeling concern for his family.

The man took a deep breath and stood up. "Your brothers and their families are all well, but . . ."

"What is it?"

"Your father has been killed," he answered simply, respectfully keeping his eyes down.

Samson shook his head in disbelief. "There must be a mistake," he mumbled almost incoherently. "He can't be dead. I just saw him . . ." Samson realized he couldn't remember the last time he had seen his family. His anger started to rise, and he stood up, making everyone nearby obviously nervous. "Did you say he was killed?" he asked pacing. "What happened? Who did this?"

"I don't have the details, sir. All I know is the Philistines in Gaza somehow found out your family lives in Zorah. They went from house to house until they found your parents." The man swallowed deeply when he saw the rage building on Samson's face. "Your mother was also injured. I was sent to ask you to come home as soon as you can." He finished the message quickly.

The long-suppressed rage erupted out of Samson. "How did the Philistines find out where my family lives? I don't know anyone in Gaza! I've never even been that far south!" He kicked a rock but continued pacing in spite of the pain it must have caused in his foot. "This must be a mistake! It can't be my father. He's never caused trouble in his life. He's always cooperated with the Philistines. They wouldn't have killed him."

"Samson, sit down and take a breath," Eli said tentatively. "There's nothing you can do right now. Let's go home and get some rest; you can leave for Zorah in the morning."

"No!" Samson thundered. "I'm leaving now. I have to get back to my family. I've been hiding here long enough."

"The sun will be down soon. You can't travel at night. There are wild animals out there; there may be soldiers waiting for you on the road. It's not safe."

Samson laughed without humor. "I dare any lion or Philistine to come at me right now!" He gathered his robe between his legs and tucked it into his belt so he could move more freely. "Goodbye, Eli. I'm going home. You should do the same." Without even looking over his shoulder, he began running toward the hills of Zorah.

Throughout the night, he continued to run. He only stopped once in the town of Bethel to draw water from the well; then he continued without rest. He reached Zorah before dawn the next morning. Even in the darkness, he could see the destruction that had been done to his family's home. The fields had all been burned, and the animal enclosure was completely empty. Before he was close enough to enter the house, he was greeted by his brother Elihu, who had been sitting watch in the family courtyard.

"Samson, I'm so glad to see you. How did you get here so quickly? We just sent the messenger two days ago." The brothers embraced and walked toward the house.

"You look exhausted, Elihu. Have you slept at all?"

"Not much. Hosah, Aaron, and I have been keeping watch around the clock since the Philistines left. Our wives have been taking turns sitting with Mother. She's been quite sick since we buried Father. I'm sorry we didn't wait for you. We didn't know you would get here so fast." Elihu led Samson into the quiet house. The two men peeked into the back room where their mother slept. Her daughter-in-law sat on the mat next to her. When she saw Samson, a flood of relief washed over her tired face. "Mother just fell asleep," she whispered. "Maybe you two should sit outside and get the fire started for breakfast. I'll come get you when she wakes up." She smiled at Samson "We're glad you're home, brother."

The two men went outside and sat by the cold stove. "What happened, Elihu?" Samson whispered.

"I still don't really know." He sighed as he went through the routine of starting a fire. "The Philistine soldiers came to the door one morning. We thought they had come for their tribute and taxes, but they dragged all of us outside and started questioning us."

"What were they asking?"

"They wanted to know if we knew you and if we were related. They said someone in Gaza had told them that your family lives in Zorah. I later found out they burned several other houses throughout the hills trying to find us."

"What did you tell them?"

"None of us spoke. They kept us at sword's point while they beat Father, but none of us said a word. Then they started pushing Mother around, and something in Father finally snapped. He picked himself up from the dust and stood toe to toe with the commander. He looked him straight in the face and told him that his son Samson would put an end to all the Philistines." Elihu's voice broke, and he was quiet for a moment. "Then the commander cut him down right in front of all of us."

Samson put his hand on his brother's shoulder. "Oh, Elihu, I'm so sorry." Tears flowed freely into his beard.

Elihu hung his head and continued miserably. "All we could do was watch while they beat Mother and killed Father. Then they burned the fields and took every animal we had."

"Were any of the wives and children taken?" Samson asked.

"No. I don't understand why they left the rest of us unharmed. Especially once Father confirmed that we are related to you. The only thing I can think of is that they are using us as a trap to try to catch you. I hesitated in sending a messenger, because I didn't know if you should come.

But Mother said she wanted you home. She said Yahweh would take care of you. I don't know if she'll survive, and I didn't want to disobey her dying request to see you. Please forgive me if I did the wrong thing."

"No," Samson said as he stood up and started pacing. "You didn't do anything wrong. I'm glad you sent for me. I should have come home a long time ago. I was wrong to hide out in Shiloh, trying to avoid what I know I'm supposed to confront. Let them come. Let them try to hurt this family again." His grief and regret melted together and fueled the familiar flame of anger that was always there smoldering just under the surface.

Just then, Elihu's wife stepped outside. "Samson, your mother is awake, and she's asking for you."

"Try to be calm, Samson," Elihu warned before his brother went into the house. "She's very frail. You don't want to cause her any extra stress."

Samson nodded and stepped into the house where he found his mother propped up on her sleeping mat. He sat next to her and let his breath out slowly as he studied the injuries on her face. Her left cheek was bruised and her eye was swollen shut. Her lip had been split open and her arm was tied securely to her body by a strip of cloth.

"What did they do to you, Mother?" he asked shakily.

"It's not serious. Elihu thinks my arm is broken, so they're trying to keep it still. The rest of it is just a little tender."

Samson clenched his fists and tried to control his anger. *What kind of monsters could do this to an old woman?* Sarai sensed his anger and patted his knee with her good hand. "It's really not as bad as it looks. I'll be all right," she smiled, making the cut on her lip tighten.

He laid his head on her lap, and she stroked his long hair.

"I'm so sorry I wasn't here to protect you, Mother. I'm sorry I let them do this to you . . . and Father," he sobbed into her blanket.

"There now," she soothed his pain away with her small hand. "Your father died bravely. I've never been more proud of him in my life. You should have seen him stand up to that Philistine officer."

"But they killed him for it," Samson choked out.

"Yes, they did. But you know what gives me comfort?" Samson raised his head and looked into her eyes. "He died in the exact place where the Lord visited us and ascended into heaven after He told us that you would be born. You know the place? Right near the family altar. I don't know if that is what gave him the strength he needed to stand up to the Philistines, or if he just finally had had enough. Either way, I felt God's presence again just as surely as I did the day He stood before me in the center of the flames."

"I wish I could feel God's presence," Samson whispered. "All I feel is hatred and anger. It's consuming me."

"Perhaps what you're feeling is Yahweh's anger and hatred toward the Philistines and what they are doing to His people. Maybe it's a gift—like your strength. Maybe you need that anger to motivate you to free our people."

Samson nodded and held his mother's hand. He felt ashamed of himself for wasting so much time. He had been trying for years to douse the flames inside of him when he should have been taking action to make changes. That explained why he never felt satisfied sitting at the gates acting as a judge. He was meant to be a warrior not a figurehead.

He watched as his mother dozed off to sleep. In his mind, he planned his attack on the Philistines of Gaza.

CHAPTER 49

Samson stayed with his family while his mother recovered from her injuries. He and his brothers kept a close eye on the area surrounding their home. There were small groups of soldiers positioned around their home, constantly watching them from a distance, but they didn't seem to be in any hurry to make a move. Samson walked to the homes scattered throughout Zorah and tried to rally the people so they could fortify and protect themselves from future attacks, but the people were bitter and hopeless. Most of them had lost a great deal at the hands of the Philistines when they came looking for Samson. They had no intentions of doing anything to help protect him or his family. Samson realized he was on his own once again.

Most of the family's food had been taken or destroyed, so Samson knew he would have to go to the nearest town to get supplies soon. He considered sending his brothers, but he knew the soldiers would never allow them to pass. He was afraid of what would happen to his family when he was gone, but he couldn't let them starve. All he could do was pray that God would protect them while he was away. He told his brothers that he was going to leave for Eshtaol before dawn and that he would be back before sunset. They found an old horn that their father had carved for them when they were children. Elihu was instructed to blow the horn at any sign of danger, and Samson would return as soon as he could. Both men knew he would not be able to hear the horn more than a mile away, but they had no choice.

Early the next morning, Samson slipped out of the house. His youngest brother, Aaron, was sitting watch on a large rock just outside of the courtyard.

"There is a group of soldiers in plain sight to the southwest. There are probably more that I can't see to the north," Aaron said as he came down from his perch. "They must know we need food. They're surely waiting for one of us to come through their lines."

"I'm sure they hope it isn't me," Samson replied confidently. "I'll see you soon."

He quickly and quietly made his way toward the familiar road to Eshtaol. He had made the journey so many times that he could do it in his sleep. The only question he had was if he should travel by road where he was sure to meet soldiers or if he should take the longer route through the trees and hidden paths. He decided to face the Philistines head on. He didn't have a bit of fear for himself, but he was worried about staying away from his family for too long. The shorter, more-direct route would certainly lead him to some kind of confrontation with the soldiers, but at least he could get it over with and get home. When he was only about a mile and a half from the town of Eshtaol, he was stopped by three armed Philistines on horseback. The leader drew his sword and held it in front of Samson's face.

"Where do you think you're going?" he asked, showing only a little bit of fear behind his cold eyes.

"I'm going to Eshtaol to get food for my family," Samson responded without flinching. "You took everything they have, or don't you remember?"

"Of course I remember. We've actually been expecting you. This is the only road to Eshtaol, and we knew you would have to pass this way sooner or later." The soldier smiled down at Samson revealing a mouth full of yellow teeth. "I should probably thank you for all you and your family are doing for my career. Dagon must be favoring me greatly. First I had the privilege of killing your father, and now I get to kill you."

Samson clenched his fists, but his face remained perfectly calm. "If you're so eager to kill me, why don't you get off of your horse and face me like a man?"

The soldier thought for a moment while his two subordinates watched and waited to see if he would accept the challenge. Eventually, he dismounted and stepped toward Samson with his sword drawn. The other two soldiers stayed close as their horses neighed and shifted nervously. Before anyone could act, Samson clapped his palms on either side of the blade and pulled it out of his opponent's hands. In one smooth motion, he flipped the sword into the air, catching it by the hilt. Blood flowed freely from his hands, but he felt nothing but power surging through his veins. He jabbed at the horse on his left who threw his rider into the dust and galloped off. The rider on the right swung his sword at Samson's head, but he was easily blocked.

As Samson fought with the Philistine sword, he remembered his cousin Joel and how he was killed by these uncircumcised dogs. He thought of his father lying dead near the family altar. He thought of his frail, injured mother in her bed at home. The anger and rage pumped through his veins as he thrust blow after blow at the soldiers in front of him. The last man on horseback tried to attack him from above, but Samson easily pulled the young soldier off of his mount and stabbed him through the heart. His partner attacked from behind, but Samson spun around and blocked the soldier's sword with the one he had taken from the commander. When he was able to switch to an offensive position, he swung his sword toward the blade of the young Philistine, and with his superhuman strength, he sliced the iron blade in half. The soldier stood paralyzed in fear, looking at what was left of the broken sword in his hand. When he finally composed himself, he thrust the jagged remains of the sword at Samson, who swung one more time, completely knocking the weapon away. He easily disposed of the second young soldier and then turned to face the man who had killed his father. The seasoned soldier scrambled on his hands and knees to take the sword of his fallen subordinate. Once he was armed, he stood to face Samson.

"Now, what were you saying about my father?" Samson asked as he held his bloodied sword up in front of him. He saw obvious fear in his opponent's eyes.

"I was just following orders," the commander stammered.

"Whose orders?"

"The Lord Maoch of Gaza sent us here to find your family. He commanded us to kill them and find you. We left most of your family alive, hoping you would come to defend them."

"Well, here I am. What do you plan to do about it?"

The soldier swallowed hard and tried to swing at Samson, but he completely missed. "I will take you back to Gaza and turn you over to the Lord Maoch." The man's voice was high and tight.

Samson swung the sword at the Philistine, hitting him on the left shoulder. The man cringed in pain but held his position.

"No, I have a better idea," Samson said. "You'll go tell your men to return to Gaza today. Tell your lord that I will be paying him a visit as soon as I have taken care of the needs of my family." He casually swung again and connected with the soldier's right thigh.

The man dropped to his knee, but quickly recovered. He swung madly at the air trying to hit Samson, but he was blocked at every attempt.

"You will tell your men to stay away from Zorah, or I will make them sorry they ever lived." He jabbed again, this time stabbing the large muscle at the top of the man's right arm, causing him to drop his sword.

"Aren't you going to kill me?" the man asked as he looked up pathetically at Samson.

"If I kill you, you're nothing more than another dead Philistine at my feet. If I let you live, you will have to go back to your people shamed and dishonored." Samson sliced the man's right cheek then threw his sword to the ground and grabbed his opponent by the neck. He felt the Philistine's pulse pound under his thumb as he squeezed tighter. The soldier gasped and kicked wildly. As soon as he stopped fighting, Samson tossed him onto the ground, where he coughed and vomited into the dust.

"I think I'll let you live for now," Samson said, towering over the soldier who quivered in fear at his feet. "You will remind your men that they are dealing with a servant of the true God of heaven." He picked him up by the back of his armor and slung him over his horse. "Tell them to stay away from my family, or they will have to deal with my God directly." He turned the horse around and slapped it on the rump, sending it running back toward Zorah. "I'll see you in Gaza!" Samson shouted after the soldier. "I'm looking forward to meeting your lord!"

Samson grabbed the reins of the remaining horse and struggled to mount it. He had never ridden anything larger than a donkey, so it took him several tries to get onto the animal's back. He was glad the ride to Eshtaol was a short one. He was eager to slide off the horse and get his feet back on solid ground. As awkward as he may have felt riding, his appearance in town was quite impressive. The townspeople knew at once that the bloodied Hebrew riding a Philistine horse had to be the great Samson. He was greeted warmly and quickly invited to the home of one of the town elders. Once he was comfortably seated, one of the daughters of the house washed his feet while another tended to his sliced palms. The two young women hand-fed him thick lentil stew with bread. He didn't bother to mention that his hands didn't hurt at all and that he was perfectly capable of feeding himself.

The townspeople gave him everything he needed for his family and sent him away, promising to check in on them periodically throughout the winter to make sure that they had enough to live on. Samson thanked them sincerely and rode awkwardly back home on the Philistine horse. It was well before sunset when he arrived, and he was relieved to find nothing had been harmed while he was away.

His nephews were the first to run out to greet him. They were impressed with his new horse, but they kept a respectful distance from the huge beast. His three brothers came out and helped him dismount and secure the animal in the empty enclosure. They all took turns slapping him on the back and welcoming him home. Even though he had only been gone a few hours, they were all very relieved to be safely reunited.

At dinner that evening, Samson told them about his encounter with the three Philistines. He informed them that he was going to Gaza to find the lord who seemed to be commanding the army from the south. His sisters-in-law shared their concern for the family's safety while he was away, but Samson assured them that the Philistines would not be bothering them again. His mother nodded in agreement. "Yes, you will go and we will be just fine here," she said. "Our God is big enough to protect us all."

CHAPTER 50

Samson packed a bag of food, put on his best robe, and mounted the horse after a few clumsy slips. He considered walking, but since he had never traveled as far south as Gaza, he decided he would use the horse as much as possible.

Rather than traveling through the now familiar Philistine towns along the coast, Samson thought it would be better to use the Judean wilderness instead. He stopped for the night in a small village just west of Debir, where he was given the appropriate hospitality. In the morning, he stiffly limped over to the horse, dreading the thought of having to ride it again. Instead, he decided to sell the animal to an Egyptian merchant for twenty-five pieces of silver. Satisfied with his deal, he proceeded to Gaza on foot.

By late afternoon, he reached the Philistine city. He stood back in amazement, taking in the huge stone wall that surrounded the perimeter. The only way into the city was through one set of gates at the eastern end of town. He had spent enough time at the gates of Shiloh to know how they worked. It was just two large wooden gates that pivoted on wooden rods at either end. At night, they would be held in place by a lock so no one could come in or out without a key. Though in principle, the gate was the same as any other, this one was larger than any he had ever seen. The walls were also thicker and stronger than any of the other Philistine towns he had visited. Unless someone was willing to swim across the Great Sea and slip in on the western side, there was no choice but to go through the gate. The opening was only about ten feet wide, so there was a line of people waiting to get through. Samson took his place behind a group of camel traders from Egypt. He listened to their strange language and watched the soldiers at the head of the line as he tried to prepare himself for the trouble he knew was about come. When he reached the gate, the soldiers studied him carefully. He felt absolutely no fear as they talked quietly among themselves. He kept his breathing slow and calm and watched every move they made, just waiting for the signal to fight. His muscles twitched in anticipation, but the signal never came. He was sure they knew him, but they had no intention of stopping him. Instead, the soldier in charge walked up to him and bowed slightly.

"Welcome to Gaza, Samson," he said respectfully. "We've been expecting you."

It wasn't the first time he had been allowed to walk right into a Philistine city. He knew most of the soldiers feared him, but he was surprised he would receive this kind of welcome after the threats he had made to their ruler.

"Where is your lord Maoch?" Samson asked the accommodating guard.

"Perhaps you will find him at Dagon's temple. He has something very special planned for you."

Samson was sure he was walking into some kind of trap, but he really didn't care. He was confident that he could handle anything they threw at him.

Samson spent a few hours strolling through the streets of Gaza. The marketplace was set up the same as most other towns, but the goods sold were far more exotic and rare. Egyptians filled the streets, buying and selling things that Samson couldn't even identify. Horses were much more common here, and he realized he probably would have gotten a better price for his Philistine horse if he would have sold it farther north. As Samson casually ambled through the market, he knew he was being watched. There were several soldiers shadowing every move he made. At one booth, Samson bought a sack of figs and snacked on them as he walked. Just for fun, he would occasionally toss a few to the soldiers and laugh at the surprised looks on their faces. He actually enjoyed toying with them.

He finally left the market and decided that he would try to find Dagon's temple and whatever waited there for him. He asked for directions and easily found the huge white building that dominated the western side of the city. As he moved closer, he found himself in a crowd of worshipers outside of the largest temple he had ever seen. He was reminded of Dagon's temple in Timnah that he had visited years earlier.

Without thinking, he again allowed himself to be washed into the building by the flood of people. Inside, he could feel the cold stone under his feet and smell incense burning in the air. The building was made up of a large center room where Dagon's statue sat surrounded by priests and priestesses performing various duties. Large white columns held up a second story where more worshipers were gathered to have an unobstructed view of their stone god. Even though the fish-god was nothing in Samson's eyes, he did have to admit the temple was impressive. As he stood mesmerized between two pillars, a woman's voice interrupted his thoughts.

"Are you lost?" she asked kindly.

Samson turned to look at the strangely familiar woman. "No, I uh . . ."

"You must be lost," she smiled. "You're a Hebrew. I can tell by the tassels on your robe. Most Hebrews at least take off their tassels before they come in here."

"Do I know you?" Samson asked, feeling confused and disoriented. Maybe it was the crowd or the thick incense in the air, but suddenly he felt like he couldn't breathe.

"I don't think so. You're much too young for me." She laughed and her voice sounded like tinkling bells.

"Timnah!" he exclaimed. "You used to work at the temple in Timnah!"

She smiled like she had just solved a riddle. "You couldn't be the same little boy with long hair that I helped all those years ago?" She reached out and caressed his braids. "Yes, it is you, but you're all grown up." She moved closer, and Samson could feel the warmth of her body against his arm. "It's too bad I'm so old. I've been given other duties to perform. But, I have someone I'd like you to meet." She took his hand and led him to a back door of the temple.

Once the door closed behind them, it was suddenly quiet. She led him down a corridor that was lined with torches and doors. She stopped in front of one of the doors and knocked softly. A young woman answered, and Samson gasped when he saw her. She looked exactly like the older woman by his side had looked when he first met her as a boy.

"This is my daughter," the old priestess purred. "She'll take good care of you." She winked at the younger woman. "This man is very special. Keep him with you all night." She walked away, leaving a trail of perfume behind her.

Samson stood statue still, staring at the beautiful woman in front of him. This was the picture he had in his mind since he was a child. He could never quite explain what he was looking for in a woman, but this was it.

"Won't you come inside?" she held her hands out to him, and he allowed himself to be led in. She knelt down in front of him and unfastened his sandals. Then she walked him to a pile of cushions and sat him down like a child. He was given something to drink, and he took it without protest. Then the Philistine woman started to sway back and forth to some kind of song only she could hear. Samson was in a complete daze as he watched her dance to the silent music. Without any thought to why he was in Gaza or what this woman might do to him, he stood up and crossed the room in two deliberate steps. He took the woman in his arms and held her firmly. For a moment she looked frightened, but then she relaxed in his arms and led him back to the cushions.

CHAPTER 51

When Samson opened his eyes, the room was dark. It took him a moment to remember where he was, and when he did, he felt sick. He looked at the Philistine woman lying next to him, and he was filled with regret and self-loathing. *How could I have allowed myself to be taken in by this seductress? What have I done?* He slowly pulled his arm out from underneath her and got dressed. He opened the door and stepped out into the cold corridor. He couldn't remember the way out. He had been so enraptured by the priestess that he hadn't paid any attention to where she took him. Maybe this was the trap the lord of Gaza had planned for him. Lure him into the room of a temple prostitute and then attack him while he slept. He had to get out of the city, but first, he had to get out of this horrible building. All the doors looked the same, and he didn't dare open them for fear of what would be waiting for him inside. He hadn't felt fear like this in a very long time. Perhaps God had really left him this time. *How can I expect Him to protect and empower someone so weak? What kind of deliverer am I if I can't avoid the temptations of a woman?* He pressed his hands against his eyes, trying to blot out the reality of what he had done. He wanted to run and hide. He wanted to get out of Gaza. He didn't care about the Lord Maoch. He didn't care how the soldiers had found out where his family lived. All he wanted to do was leave this place. He felt like the stone walls of the corridor were closing in on him, and he started to run. He opened a door and found several women sleeping on the floor. He quickly closed it and ran on. He tried several other doors, but none of them led to freedom. Finally, he found the door that took him back into the temple of Dagon. The temple was empty except for the statue in the center. Samson caught his breath and tried to calm himself now that he was out in the open space.

CHAPTER 51

He walked up to the stone god and looked into its cold, dead eyes. He was thankful that he served a living God, not one made of stone. He felt his strength come back to him and he stood taller, took a deep breath, and spit in the face of the Philistine god, Dagon. He then turned and left the temple, hoping never to return.

Once he was out in the night air, he started running toward the gate. He knew it would be locked, but he also knew he had to get out before morning. If he waited, he was sure the entire Philistine army would be ready to kill him. When he reached the gate, he found two watchmen nearby sleeping soundly. Iron bars held the gate securely closed. He quickly searched for another way out, but he knew he wouldn't find one, so he went back to the gate and stood silently for a moment wondering what to do. The thin hairs on the back of his neck stood on end, and he swung around expecting to see someone or something standing behind him. But he was alone except for the sleeping guards. Then he heard a familiar Voice in the wind.

"Pull," it whispered. *"Pull."*

Samson grabbed hold of the gates, one in each hand, and he started to pull. He felt the two posts that held the gates start to give.

"Pull!" the Voice whispered more urgently.

His face turned red, and he focused every bit of strength he had into pulling the gates loose. With a crack, the posts gave way, and the huge gates broke loose in Samson's hands. The guards woke up and stared at him in shock. Samson smiled at them and heaved the gates onto his shoulders.

"Sweet dreams," he smirked as he strode away, taking with him the city's main defenses on his back.

Both men seemed immobilized, unable to call for help and unsure anyone would even believe them if they came. Samson had no fear of being followed. He walked east, back toward the land where his people lived. He carried the gates to the top of a hill overlooking the Judean town of Hebron. He threw the pile of wood and iron down to the ground and laughed. *Nothing those Philistines have can stop me. I am more powerful than any other man who has ever lived.* As Samson looked across at the hillside town of Hebron, he almost felt as though he could move the mountain underneath it if he wanted to. Gates couldn't keep him in, armies couldn't keep him out. *I am invincible,* he told himself.

Chapter 52

Samson took his time returning home. He stayed in the lands of Judah through the cold, rainy winter months. With the shepherds staying close to home, Samson was able to purchase a few animals to help rebuild his family's flock. He used some of the silver he had received from selling the Philistine horse, but many Israelites simply gave him the best of their herds to show their appreciation and respect for all he had done to their oppressors. In Bethlehem, a feast was prepared in his honor, and the townspeople presented him with a young ram, two ewes, and a doe goat. They also laid a table of food before him that was better than he had had even at his wedding feast. It didn't take long for the people of Bethlehem to start talking about crowning Samson king. For years there had been whispers throughout the tribes of Israel that a king was needed to unite them and help them stand against the surrounding nations. Samson remembered the Levites in Shiloh trying to convince Eli that he should become king. His friend quickly declined and reminded the people that God was the Leader of His people. Samson was flattered by the esteem the Judeans held him in, but the old familiar restlessness made him uncomfortable staying in one place for too long. Something else deep within him told him he was not meant to be a ruler. He didn't want a throne or a crown—he wanted Philistine blood.

When the farmers around Bethlehem started planting their wheat and barley, Samson decided it was time to go home. He took his small flock north through the hills, eager to show his brothers what he had accumulated. When he arrived home, he found his mother sitting outside in the sun, looking smaller and frailer than when he had last seen her. The other adults were off in the field planting while Sarai looked after her grandchildren. When she saw her oldest son approach, she did not rise, but smiled lovingly up at him. His little nieces and nephews ran to him and jumped all over him, hanging from his back, legs, and arms. He playfully dragged them around, crying mercy until they finally released him, falling to the ground giggling.

Samson then went to his mother. Kneeling next to her, he kissed her softly on the head. "Are you well, Mother?"

"Yes," she replied, holding both of his hands in hers and looking up at him with so much love that Samson thought he might cry.

"I've brought home some animals," he said, motioning toward his small flock. "It's not much, but they are the best quality sheep in the country. Two of the ewes are pregnant, so we will have more lambs soon."

"God is so good to us," Sarai said softly as she looked at the animals. "I see you have a goat too! Does she have milk?"

"Yes. She produces even more than our old doe," he replied feeling very pleased with himself. "I plan to go to Mahaneh-dan and Eshtaol now that I have some money. Perhaps we can buy a few of Uncle Asahel's animals to breed with these. The ram I got in Bethlehem is very good tempered, so I hope his offspring will be easier to manage than Ra's."

Sarai smiled, remembering the old ram that had caused her husband and sons so much trouble over the years. "Do you see how Yahweh can work all things to His own good?" She had a faraway look in her eyes. "The Philistines took what we had, but He replaced it all with something even better."

Samson didn't think much about God these days, but his mother's faith made him feel warm and safe.

Just then, he heard his brothers calling to him from the field nearby.

"I'm going to take care of the animals and then see if my brothers need any help in the field. Will you be all right here?" Samson asked as he rose to his feet.

"Now that you're home, I have perfect peace," she said looking up at him. "Oh, Samson, your robe is so frayed from all your travel. I'll make you another one right away."

He looked down at his road-worn clothing and realized it was shabby. It was foolish of him to wear clothing of such fine fabric when he was traveling. A sturdy goat-hair robe would have been much more practical, but not nearly as stylish.

"No, Mother, don't trouble yourself with that. I have plenty of money. I'll just buy a new one."

"Very well," Sarai replied, looking just a little hurt. "Ask your sisters-in-law where to find a weaver who can make something large enough for you. If I remember correctly, there's a woman down in the Sorek Valley who is very talented at the loom. I believe her name is Delilah."

"*Hmmm,* Delilah." Samson liked the sound of the name. "It means 'delicate,' doesn't it?"

Sarai eyed her son suspiciously. "You know, I really wouldn't mind making the clothes myself."

"No, I think I'll just pay this Delilah a visit to see what she can weave for me." Samson kissed his mother again and left her sitting in the sun.

CHAPTER 53

The next day, Samson took his remaining silver and walked down into the Sorek Valley to find the weaver named Delilah. His sisters-in-law told him where her house was and warned him to expect to pay heavily for whatever work she did for him. He found out that Delilah was a widow who lived alone in her deceased husband's house. She was very talented on her loom, weaving patterns that no one else in the area could copy. Samson was surprised he had never heard of her before, but then he had never needed someone to make fine clothes for him in the past. For several years, his clothing had either been taken as booty from battle or given to him by grateful Israelites. Prior to that, his mother had always made him coarse, simple clothing that was practical, but not at all fitting someone of his position. Now he felt justified in purchasing something especially nice for himself. He was, after all, a judge of Israel with the eyes of the nation upon him. It was about time he looked and dressed the part.

He reached Delilah's home and found her in her courtyard grinding wheat to make bread. She didn't hear him approach, so he was able to study her openly for a moment. Her head was uncovered like most of the Philistine women, and her raven-black hair was loosely pulled back from her face. Her small hands worked quickly and efficiently, and she seemed completely engrossed in the work in front of her.

Samson cleared his throat to get her attention. She looked up startled and pushed the loose strands of hair away from her face. That's when Samson got his first look at her face. To say she was beautiful would be like saying the sun setting into the Great Sea was nice. Samson's breath caught in his throat.

"Can I help you?" she asked, looking slightly annoyed with the interruption of her work.

"I, uh, I'm looking for the weaver Delilah," he stammered.

"Well, you found her," she replied smiling slightly. She stood up and wiped her hands on the front of her robe. "What can I do for you?"

"I need some new clothes."

She eyed him up and down. "Well, you're a big one, aren't you?" She looked amused. "I don't have anything already made that will fit you. I'd have to weave something especially for you. It will be pretty expensive. Do you have money?"

"Of course I have money," Samson said, feeling offended. He jingled the purse attached to his girdle.

Delilah slowly walked around him, sizing him up. "For an ordinary-sized man, it would cost five pieces of silver for the simplest robe I can make. But you're not normal sized, and I don't think you want anything simple, do you?"

Samson couldn't respond. Her open appraisal made him very uncomfortable.

"Yes, I think for you it will cost twenty pieces of silver."

"What? That's ridiculous! I won't pay more than ten." He knew the bartering game well enough to play.

She pretended defeat and backed away. "Well, then I guess you'll have to settle for one of the other weavers in town. I'm sure they can make you a lovely camel-and-goat-hair cloak that will make you look just like all the other simple Hebrews."

He smiled at her in amusement. He was too old and too seasoned to be taken in by her sales strategy. "Well, then, I guess you don't want to make clothes for the great Samson of Zorah. I'm sure I won't have trouble finding someone else to make something for the man who could be the first king of Israel."

"You're Samson?" she replied, looking appropriately impressed. "The same Samson who pulled the city gates right out of the wall in Gaza?"

"That's right," he said proudly. "Now, do you think you have the skill required to make something for me?"

"Of course I have the skills," she said, regaining her composure. "The question is, does the great Samson have the money?"

The two stood face-to-face, eyeing each other like combatants on the field of battle.

"I'll pay fifteen pieces of silver, but it had better be the best clothing you've ever made."

She smiled triumphantly. "Very well. I'll do it for fifteen, and I'll get started right away. I'll have to measure you. You're much larger than the other men I make clothes for."

Samson's heart fluttered at the way she boldly studied him. She went into the house, leaving him alone in the courtyard. He wasn't sure what to do with himself, but she quickly returned, holding a long rope in her hands.

"Put your arms out," she ordered.

"Why, what do you plan to do with that rope?"

"I'm going to measure you, silly," she giggled quietly. "What did you think I was going to do, tie you up?"

He smiled and held his arms out to the side. She reached around him, sliding the rope behind his back. Her body was pressed up against his for a moment as she pulled the rope together in front of his chest. His pulse raced but he kept his gaze straight ahead. She marked the rope then moved it down to his waist. She moved her hands freely over his body. Every brush of her fingers over the bare skin at his neck and wrists sent heat surging through him. Occasionally, she would look up at him and smile knowingly. She seemed to enjoy torturing him.

"There, I think I have all the measurements I need," she started to say, but Samson grabbed her and pulled her close to him. He kissed her firmly then stepped back and took a deep breath.

"When will the clothing be ready?" he asked shakily.

"Come back in three days," she said smiling and smoothing her hair. "I should have something ready for you by then."

CHAPTER 54

When Samson returned three days later, he saw soldiers just a short distance away from Delilah's house. They were a common enough sight, but he wondered why they would be watching her house so intently. He laughed to himself and waved at the men in the distance. They looked away nervously as though they hadn't seen him.

When he reached her courtyard, he found her playing a harp and humming a strange song. She looked up at him and smiled. When she rose to meet him, it was obvious she had taken some time and care in dressing herself that morning. Her hair had been brushed so that it shone like onyx, and her deep purple robe lay loosely over the curves of her body. Everything about her looked soft and flowing, making him want to touch her more than he had ever wanted anything in his life. He inwardly scolded himself for stupidly falling for yet another Philistine woman. He couldn't let her get to him like the others had.

"I've been waiting for you," she said as she walked toward him. "Come inside and see what I have done so far." She led him into her house, which was surprisingly large and richly decorated. He wondered how a widow woman was able to live so comfortably. Samson's eyes wandered around the living area. There was a table in the center of the room with cushions placed around it and dishes stacked neatly at the corner. A brightly colored curtain separated the back part of the house.

"What's back there?" he asked absently.

"Just some extra rooms. I don't use that part of the house now that my husband is dead."

"It looks like you've recently had guests." Samson said as he inspected the large table.

"Would you be surprised to know that the lords from each of the five

Philistine cities came to dine with me just yesterday?"

"You must be pretty important then," he said as he continued to scan the room. In one corner stood a large horizontal loom with what was probably the beginning of his cloak stretched out between the four stakes that were solidly planted into the dirt floor. Not far from the loom was a mat that had been folded and tucked away into a sleeping shelf built into the wall. His eyes lingered just a little too long on her bed. Delilah followed his gaze and smiled knowingly at him. He blushed and tried to keep his eyes averted so she couldn't see the effect she had on him.

"I haven't finished the cloak yet, but here's your tunic." She handed the soft cloth to him. Samson took the garment from her. Even though he was a grown man, he still felt slightly embarrassed having this woman touching his undergarments.

"I haven't cut the neck opening yet. I wanted you to see that no one else has worn it . . . I have the impression that you don't trust me." She smiled playfully as she picked up her shears. "If you're satisfied, I'll cut it now."

Samson inspected the tunic. She stepped closer, turning the sharp shears in her hands. In one graceful motion, she took the tunic from him and expertly cut the neck opening.

"Here, why don't you try it on?" she handed it back to him when she was finished. When she saw the blush on his face, she giggled and turned to leave. "Don't worry, as much as I'd like to, I won't watch."

After she left him alone in her house, it took him a few minutes to regain his composure. He tried on the tunic and found it to be softer and nicer than any garment he had ever owned. If she could do this with his undergarment, what could she do with the outer cloak? He left the new tunic on and quickly covered it with his old robe. He bundled up his old tunic and hid it under his arm then he went outside to face the woman again.

"It's very nice," he said simply. "When will you have the cloak finished?"

"Just a few more days. I have a good start on it already. Let me show you what is already woven." She led Samson back inside. "Come back in one week, and I'll have it finished—that is, unless you would like to stay with me to supervise my work."

"No, I have to be going. The sheep need to be sheared, and my family still has planting to do. I really should be there to help."

"You don't mean to tell me that the great Samson tends sheep and works in the fields like a common farmer?" she asked, sounding surprised. "You're practically a king! You should be enjoying life." She walked to the table and poured two cups of wine. "If you were like our Philistine lords, you would stay and have a drink with me. *They* weren't in such a hurry to leave."

Her words pricked his pride and jealousy, so he roughly took the cup from her. Samson wasn't afraid of breaking his Nazirite vow anymore. Somehow he seemed to have forgotten that all of his great deeds were not his own doing. He drained the cup and then sat down on a cushion next to her fire pit. *This girl doesn't frighten me,* Samson told himself. *What can she do to me? I am Samson, the killer of lions, the destroyer of armies! And I* am *practically a king.* He had more important things to do than work with his family on the tedious jobs of common people. They would be just fine without him. Maybe he could just stay for a few hours, and then he could go home after everyone had their midday rest, and he would be ready to work.

Delilah sat down next to him, so close that her shoulder and thigh touched his. She poured him another drink and smiled up at him in the most enchanting way. "There now, that's better," she purred. "Just relax and spend a little time with me. I'm not going to hurt you."

CHAPTER 55

Samson did stay with Delilah until his cloak was finished. He told himself he wanted to make sure she did a good job, but they both knew why he was really there. It took her twice as long to finish as she said it would, but Samson didn't mind. In fact, he was almost disappointed when she told him that the job was done. Samson inspected the richly patterned clothes and found them to be flawless. He paid her the fifteen pieces of silver that they had agreed upon. At first, she was delighted to receive the money, but then her mood suddenly turned.

"You're not going to leave me now, are you?" she asked pouting.

"Well, you're finished with my clothes. I don't have any other reason to stay, do I?"

She slapped him and threw herself down on a cushion, crying. "How can you say that? Don't I mean anything at all to you? Just because I'm not an Israelite doesn't mean you can take advantage of me and leave."

"What do you want me to do, marry you?"

Bitter tears streamed down her face as she looked up at him. "I don't need a husband! In case you haven't noticed, I'm doing just fine on my own."

"Well then, what do you want from me?" he asked helplessly. He had grown to care for her, and he hated the thought of now sleeping alone, but he wasn't about to allow this Philistine temptress to trap him like the others had.

"Just stay with me," she cried pathetically. "Let me get to know you."

"You already know me."

"No, I don't! You don't tell me anything about yourself. You say you love me, but those are just words. Real lovers share everything with each other."

He reluctantly sat down next to her and stroked her soft black hair. The smell of her perfume intoxicated him.

"I do love you, Delilah. What do you want me to do to prove it to you?"

She smiled through her tears and took him in her arms, kissing him softly. "Just stay with me, Samson. Let me get to know you better. Trust me and open up to me."

Samson yielded to her kisses and sank deeper into her arms.

"Tell me the secret of your strength," she whispered between kisses.

At first he wasn't sure she had even spoken, so he didn't answer, but then she stopped kissing him and looked directly into his eyes. "If you really love and trust me, you'll tell me what makes you so strong."

He pulled back from her and took a deep breath, trying to cool the fire she had started in him.

"Why do you want to know that?" he asked suspiciously.

"Because I want to know if you truly love me," she said trying to sound casual.

Samson was no fool. He knew why the Philistine lords had come to visit her and why the soldiers were always watching her house from a distance. They had tried everything else to catch him, and now they were trying to use the wiles of this woman. He wondered what they had offered her. Had they threatened her like they had Peles? No, Delilah was not one to be threatened—not even by Philistine soldiers and lords. He stood up and started pacing. He felt as though the walls were closing in on him, and he had to go outside.

"Samson!" she called after him. "Don't go."

He slammed the door behind him and walked around the house, scanning the area for soldiers. They tried to hide, but his keen eyes had no trouble spotting them.

"All right," he said more to himself than to the soldiers who were much too far away to hear him. "You think you can trap me? After everything I've done, you think you have anything strong enough to hold me?" He paced back and forth, ranting into the open air. "I'll play your little game, you Philistine dogs! You have to send a woman to do your work—fine! I can handle her too. Don't you know yet that there is nothing you can do to defeat me?" He took a deep breath and walked back to the front of the house. Delilah was there looking pale and frightened. When she saw him, she threw herself into his arms.

"I'm sorry, Samson!" she sobbed. "Please don't leave me. I love you! I need you to stay with me!" Her tears soaked the front of his new cloak, stirring in him a mixture of pity and disgust.

"You want to know the secret of my strength?" he asked, holding her out at arm's length.

Her eyes were wide, and Samson knew he had her full attention. "All you have to do is tie me up with seven fresh vines that have never been dried, and I will become as weak as any other man."

"Is that all?" Delilah asked, sniffling.

"Yes, that's all." He smiled down at her. "I need to take a walk. Why don't you make dinner. I'll be back in a few hours."

"Do you promise you'll come back?" she whimpered.

"Of course," he replied. Then he added with a smirk, "Don't you trust me?"

CHAPTER 56

Samson walked through the valley toward the familiar hillside paths of his childhood home. He didn't want to see his family because he knew they would only inundate him with questions about where he had been the last few weeks. He just wanted to be alone. He needed time to think—and time to allow Delilah to set her trap. After all these years, after everything the Philistines had done to try to defeat him, it all came back to a woman. He remembered Peles and the way she cried and pleaded with him to tell her the answer to his riddle. Even though she managed to get him to tell, the Philistines still ended up losing the battle. *When are they going to learn that it doesn't matter what they do to me? They can never beat me,* Samson told himself. Although he looked forward to the fight that was sure to be waiting for him when he returned, he couldn't help but feel a little angry with Delilah. She was beautiful, but he didn't love her. How could he love someone who was trying to trap him? He was glad he had lied to her. She didn't deserve the truth. He couldn't wait to see her face when he snapped the vines she was sure to tie him with. He couldn't wait to snap the necks of the Philistines who were sure to be waiting for him. His heart pounded with anticipation.

After two long hours, he returned to Delilah's house. His trained eye saw men's footprints in the sand outside her door. He could smell them waiting for him behind the curtain to the back room. When he walked into her home, she rose nervously to meet him.

"I have dinner ready outside. Would you like to eat out there or in here at the table?"

"I'm not hungry," Samson said as he crossed the room and took her in his arms. He may not have been in love with her, but he certainly liked the way she felt next to him.

"Wait, Samson," she said breathlessly as she pulled herself free from his grasp. "Let me get you something to drink. You must be thirsty from all that walking." She poured him a glass of wine and led Samson to a pile of cushions in the corner. "Just sit down and relax. Let me wash the dirt from your feet." She knelt in front of him and untied his sandals. Samson drank his wine and leaned against the wall. He closed his eyes enjoying the feeling of her hands and hair on his feet. While she washed and rubbed his feet, she hummed a soft strange tune that made Samson unexplainably sleepy. When she was finished, she took the cup from his hands and held it to his lips so he could drink again. Then she curled up next to him, humming softly until Samson drifted off into a deep sleep.

"Samson!" he heard her yelling sometime later. "Wake up!"

He didn't know how long he had been asleep, but it was now completely dark outside. He slowly opened his eyes and found her standing over him looking excited and afraid all at the same time.

"What is it?" he mumbled groggily.

"It's the Philistines! They're here for you!"

Samson instantly woke up and realized his hands and feet had been tied with seven green vines. Several soldiers burst out of the back room of her house and came toward him. Samson easily broke the vines just as he knew he would. In the moment he had before the Philistines were on him, he looked at Delilah, whose face had turned ashen. He smiled at her and winked before he grabbed hold of the closest man and cracked his neck with one hand. When the others saw that Samson still had his strength, they scrambled out of the house as quickly as they could. He was able to grab two more men as they were on their way out the door. When the soldiers were gone, Samson turned to Delilah and crossed his arms over his chest. She cowered in the farthest corner of the room.

"I . . . I didn't know they would try to . . ." she stammered.

"You didn't know they were here? You didn't know they would try to capture me once you tied me up with the vines they brought for you?" He walked toward the cushions he had been sleeping on and scooped up his sandals that were still lying on the floor. "What did they offer you, Delilah?"

She tried to move toward the door, but he blocked her path. "Was it jewels? Land? No, it was money, wasn't it? More money so you can continue living your wealthy lifestyle without having to slave over your loom every day. Well, my delicate little Delilah, your plan didn't work, did it?"

He stood directly in front of her and held her chin roughly in his hand.

"I thought you said you loved me," she whimpered. "Why did you lie to me?"

He laughed and released her. "And what if I would have told you the truth? What if I would have told you how to make me as weak as any other man?" He thought for a moment. "You know what, it wouldn't even matter. There's nothing you or anyone else can do to me!" He turned and walked out of her house and into the pitch blackness outside.

"Samson, wait. Please don't leave. I'm sorry I betrayed you. I still love you!"

When he didn't stop walking, she called after him. "You'll be back! I know you'll come back to me!"

Somewhere deep inside, Samson knew she was right.

CHAPTER 57

When Samson returned home, he found most of the work had been finished without him. He was right; they really didn't need him. His youngest brother had taken the small flock out to graze. His middle brother had left with his family to help in the fields of Mahaneh-dan. Only Elihu and the women and children were left. His mother examined him with curious eyes, but no one asked him where he had been. His sister-in-law admired his new robe.

"She's very talented, isn't she?"

"Yes," Samson replied moodily. "She has many talents."

"She didn't sew the tassels onto your new clothes though. Would you like me to do it for you?"

Somehow Samson had completely forgotten the tassels he had worn on his clothing almost every day of his life. "Yes, sister. I would appreciate that," he answered as he sat down and took a small loaf of bread from the basket near his mother.

"You have a cut on your hand," Sarai observed as she took his arm and examined him. "Did you get in a fight?" Worry deepened the wrinkles on her forehead.

"Oh, it's nothing." He gently pulled his arm away from his mother. "Just a little scratch."

She looked at him suspiciously for a moment then poured him a cup of sweetened goat's milk.

"Your brother Hosah and his family are helping hoe flax for Uncle Asahel in Mahaneh-dan." Sarai talked casually as she ground a pile of grain in front of her. Samson wished she wouldn't work so hard. Her crooked hands looked painful, and he knew her arm still bothered her from time to time, but she wasn't about to slow down and leave all the work to her daughters-in-law.

"We'll be going to meet them in a few weeks; then we'll all go to Shiloh together for Passover."

"Oh no, Mother," Samson exclaimed. "You shouldn't be making such a long journey."

"Nonsense. Uncle Asahel has a donkey I can ride, so it won't be any trouble at all. Besides, I love celebrating the festivals with other believers." She tucked a stray strand of gray hair back under her head covering. "Will you be coming with us?"

Samson thought for a while. As nice as it would be to see Eli again, for some reason, the thought of being so close to God's tabernacle didn't appeal to him.

"I don't know, Mother. Maybe I'll just stay here and spend some time alone. I've been traveling for so long. I think being home would be a nice change of pace for me."

She frowned slightly, but after all these years, she knew there was no point arguing with him. "Very well. Should we leave the flock with you or take them to Mahaneh-dan to stay with the hired boy?"

"Take them with you," Samson replied, feeling just a little bit guilty. "You know how unpredictable my life is. I never know when I may have to leave. I would hate to leave the flock without a shepherd." Inwardly he knew he could never stay home for so long. He didn't know where he would go after his family left, but a picture of Delilah kept filling his mind.

For the next several weeks, he helped his family around the house and counted the days until they would leave for Mahaneh-dan. Even though his brothers had expanded the family garden to an impressive collection of small fields, there still wasn't enough work to keep him busy.

He thought about Delilah constantly. Somehow the anger he felt toward her slowly disappeared until, eventually, he found the entire situation somehow amusing. He knew he would go to her as soon as he could.

Finally the day came when his family packed up and headed north. When they were out of sight, he extinguished the fire in the oven, secured the house, and headed west toward the Sorek Valley. As he walked, he thought about what kind of greeting he would receive when he saw Delilah again. Maybe he should have brought a gift for her. What could he give her that she would want? She would laugh at him if he brought her an animal, and he didn't have any silver left to buy her something. He would just have to go to her empty-handed and hope that she would take him back. Then he remembered—she was the one who had betrayed him. He owed her nothing. She should be grateful to have him return at all. Feeling more confident, he approached her house and knocked on her door. He knew she was a late sleeper, so he wasn't surprised when she answered the door looking tired and disheveled.

"Come back later," she started to say until she realized it was Samson standing in front of her. "Oh, it's you!" Her face lit up, and she reached up to embrace him. She was still warm from her bed, and her hair smelled like flowers. Samson walked into the house and closed the door behind him while she still clung to him.

"I wondered if you'd ever come back," she exclaimed, kissing him all over his bearded face. "I missed you so much."

"I missed you too," he replied honestly.

"Does this mean you forgive me?" she asked, with hope clearly written all over her face.

"Of course I forgive you. It's really kind of funny if you think about it. You should have seen your face when I broke those vines."

She didn't look amused. "How could you lie to me like that?" The joy on her face from his return had instantly vanished. "I thought you said you loved me."

"I do love you," he protested as he tried to kiss her, but she pulled away. "Come on," he pleaded with a little laugh. "I was just playing with you. Of course vines could never hold me."

"Then what will hold you?" she asked, trying to sound casual.

Surely she wasn't trying to trap him again. He thought for a moment then answered cautiously. "Vines can't hold me, but ropes—that's entirely different."

"What do you mean?" He had her complete attention.

"Well, I'm not sure if I should tell you this," he teased.

"Please Samson; you said you loved me, remember? If you love me, you'll tell me."

"All right," he answered reluctantly, trying to hide his smile. "If someone were to tie me with brand-new ropes, I would be as weak as any other man." He thought back to his battle at the Rock of Etam when the men of Judah tied him up to hand him over to the Philistines. He wondered if Delilah had ever heard the entire story. If she had, she would know immediately that he was lying.

"New ropes?" she asked suspiciously.

"That's right. But if they have ever been used on anyone else, they won't work on me."

"Is it some kind of magic?"

"Yes, that's right; it's magic." He tried hard not to laugh. "Now why don't you fix me something to eat? I haven't even had breakfast yet."

"I don't have a thing here to feed you. I wasn't expecting company." She busily combed her hair and changed her robe. "Let me run into Timnah to get a few things, and I'll come right back. I'll make a feast for you."

"You don't have to go. I'd be happy with some stale bread and your company." Samson couldn't help but feel disappointed.

She tossed him a loaf of hard bread and continued bustling around the house. "Here, this will hold you over until I get back. Just a few hours, my love, and we'll have everything we need. We won't have to leave this house for a month." She absently kissed the top of his head and turned to leave. "I'll be back soon," she called as she walked out.

Samson was left alone on her bed with nothing but a piece of hard bread to eat. He sighed deeply, knowing she was going to betray him yet again. He considered leaving, but then something inside of him longed for another battle with the Philistines—and with her. His everyday life had become too routine and dull. At least this made him feel alive. He leaned back against the wall and ate his bread then dozed off to sleep, dreaming of Delilah and a mountain of dead Philistines before him.

CHAPTER 58

When Delilah returned, she went straight to work preparing food for Samson. He woke up several hours later to find the table covered with all the finest things Timnah had to offer. The crops had not yet been harvested, but the dried fruit, roasted lamb, and soft fresh bread looked and smelled as good as anything he had ever eaten at a harvest festival. He thought of his family in Shiloh eating unleavened bread and lamb with bitter herbs, and he was glad he had decided to stay.

Delilah kept his cup full of the sweetest wine he had ever tasted. As they ate and drank, he felt more and more relaxed and comfortable. His head started to swim, and his vision became blurry, but it didn't matter. As long as he could see Delilah's beautiful face in front of him, he was content. As evening approached, Samson grew very tired. Delilah stood before him and gently led him to her bed. He could feel the warmth of her body next to him as he fell into a deep, relaxing sleep.

After what felt like minutes, he was jarred awake by Delilah's voice and the sound of men scrambling toward him.

"Samson, wake up!" she yelled as she shook him. "The Philistines are here! Wake up!"

Samson jumped to his feet feeling only slightly off balance. He looked down and saw his hands had been tied with new ropes. He pulled his arms apart and easily snapped the ropes just as he had done at the Rock of Etam. He smiled to himself as the men who were charging at him instantly changed direction and ran to the door.

"What's the matter?" he yelled. "I thought you wanted a fight!" He pretended to chase after them, but he really didn't have the energy or desire to have a real battle. Once they were gone, he collapsed back onto Delilah's bed.

"Oh, Samson," she cooed as she sat next to him stroking his long hair. "Are you all right? I had no idea they would tie you up like that while we were sleeping. I'm so glad you're safe."

He kept his head down, feeling the effects of the wine and the adrenaline pumping through him. Her hand on his hair was soothing and relaxing, causing any anger he may have had to quickly vanish at her touch.

Just as he started to doze off again, she spoke softly into his ear. "Samson, why won't you tell me the secret of your great strength? If you really loved me, you wouldn't deceive me."

He was too tired to fight with her. Her fingertips gently loosened his braids as she ran her hands through his hair. He sank deeper and deeper into her relaxing touch.

"My braids," he murmured sleepily. His eyes fluttered halfway open, and he looked at the large loom she had set up next to her bed. "If you weave the seven locks of my braids into your loom, I'll be as weak as any other man."

"Oh, Samson," she replied happily as she kissed him and continued stroking his hair. "You do love me."

Samson dozed off again. Occasionally, he felt Delilah's hands tugging and pulling at his hair, but he convinced himself that it was just a dream. When his eyes started to flutter open, she gently soothed him back to sleep. Sometime before sunrise, he woke again to the sound of her voice.

"Wake up, Samson; they're back!" she shouted.

Samson tried to raise his head from the bed, but his hair had been woven in the loom. He was able to sit up enough to see two soldiers standing cautiously in front of the door, ready to escape if necessary. They were both young men, and it was easy to see that neither one of them wanted to face him. Delilah stood nearby yelling, "Samson, can you get up?"

He smiled slyly at her then stood to his full height. Twisting his head, he was able to completely uproot her loom and pull all four of the wooden stakes right out of the ground. The effects of the wine had completely worn off, and Samson was back to his old self. He shook his head, and the wooden pieces fell at his feet. The two soldiers scrambled to get out, and Samson made no attempt to chase them. Instead, he turned to face Delilah.

"Obviously, you don't know who you're dealing with," he hissed spitefully as he kicked the pieces of her loom away from his feet. "Don't you know I killed a thousand men at the Rock of Etam with nothing more than the jawbone of a donkey? And that's after my own people tied me with new ropes that I snapped off as though they had been burned in a fire." He took a few long strides toward her, and she collapsed on the floor in front of him looking as though she feared for her life. He picked her up by her shoulders and held her in front of him. "I know you've heard the story of my pulling the gates of Gaza right out of the ground. How could you think your little loom could hold me?"

"Samson, I'm sorry," she stammered.

"Haven't you figured out I can't be defeated?" he yelled in her face.

"Please, Samson, let me go. Don't hurt me. I love you . . ."

"Enough!" he shouted, dropping her back to her feet. "Philistines don't know how to love."

"But you do, don't you?" she asked cautiously. "You love me. I know you do. I can tell when you hold me and kiss me." She carefully stepped toward him and put her hand on his face.

He backed away, trying to avoid her touch. His retreat gave her more confidence, and she moved closer. "Samson, I do love you. I just need to know that you love me too." His back was now to the wall, and she pressed herself boldly against him. She seemed quite sure now that he wasn't going to harm her.

"I hate you," he whispered, trying to keep his breathing steady.

"No, you love me. I'll prove it to you." She moved her hands freely over his body until he completely surrendered to her.

Chapter 59

Samson stayed with Delilah for several weeks, taking from her whatever she offered. At first, she avoided talking about his strength and what could be done to make him weak, but then eventually she started asking him again. It got to the point where she was hounding him constantly, trying to find out what would make him weak. He considered leaving, but the thought of sleeping alone kept him there. He tried to deceive her again with strange and elaborate tricks that could be used to bind him, but she always knew when he was toying with her, and it only made things worse. For days she cried and pleaded and treated him coldly. When he was just about to leave, she would completely change directions and shower him with affection.

When everything she had failed, she collapsed in front of him and wailed, "Why don't you love me, Samson? I do everything for you, and you can't even tell me this one little thing."

He picked her up, feeling exhausted and beaten down. Fighting a thousand men wasn't as tiring as doing battle with this one little female.

"Enough, Delilah. Why can't you just leave it alone?"

"Because I can't believe that you love me if you keep lying to me and keeping secrets from me." She clung to him, sobbing hysterically. He remembered his wife, Peles, and the way she had pleaded with him for the answer to his riddle. He had told her and it brought only ruin to her and honor to him. *Maybe if I tell Delilah the truth, it will silence her and give me peace.* Deep down, he really didn't think there was a way to make him as weak as any other man. *I have already broken my Nazirite vow so many times and am so disconnected from the God of Israel that it just doesn't matter anymore. What difference will it make if I tell her?*

CHAPTER 59

"Please, Samson, please tell me how you can be bound. If you don't, I know I'll die."

"I can't stand this anymore. Just stop. You're driving me crazy. If anyone is going to die, it's going to be me—from your constant badgering."

"But, if you would just tell me, we could be happy."

Samson pushed her away and collapsed on the bed. He couldn't take it anymore. "Fine, I'll tell you!" he exclaimed, feeling completely defeated and exhausted. She sat down next to him and looked deeply into his face as he spoke. "A razor has never touched my head," he began slowly. "I have been a Nazirite since I was in my mother's womb, which means I can't cut my hair. If I am shaved, then all of my strength will leave me, and I'll be just like any other man."

Delilah knew at once that he was telling the truth. "Oh, Samson, you do love me. Thank you for telling me." She kissed him passionately.

"I suppose you have to go to town now for some kind of errand," he said as he pushed her away. He knew the routine well enough.

"Not just yet," she said as she drew closer to him.

Later that evening, Delilah left Samson sleeping peacefully on her mat while she went to Timnah to tell the Philistine lords what she had discovered. She convinced them to bring an army and the fifty-five hundred pieces of silver they had promised her. She was sure that she finally had the answer, and now she would live the rest of her days like a queen. She hoped that somehow Samson would be able to defeat the soldiers again and come back to her, but even if he didn't, she would have enough money to be happy—even if she were alone.

She snuck back into her house with the army and the five most important men in the country waiting outside. Once she was certain Samson was fast asleep, she brought a young man in to shave off his hair while his head was resting heavily on her lap. When he was finished, the young man took his trophy of hair outside with him to show the soldiers while Delilah continued to stroke his bald head.

"Samson, wake up," she whispered as she poked him in the face.

He swatted at her hand, but she continued to poke harder and harder until his eyes were open.

"What are you doing?" he asked groggily, not even noticing that his hair was gone.

She pinched him and poked him until he was fully awake.

"What's the matter with you?" he asked trying to push her hands away. "That hurts; stop it."

"Make me," she said, sounding like a cruel child.

"Fine." He grabbed both of her wrists, but she squirmed free. He felt strange and different. Had she drugged him with one of her herbal drinks? He didn't remember drinking any wine. What was wrong with him?

She slapped him across the face, smiling bitterly at him. His hand automatically went to his cheek which felt foreign to him now that his beard was gone. "What have you done to me?" he asked.

"You're not really surprised, are you?" she asked as she slapped him again.

He grabbed her wrist, but she easily broke his grip. She smiled the most wicked, triumphant smile Samson had ever seen.

"Come on in, boys. He's all yours!" Delilah called to the men outside.

A soldier with yellow teeth and a familiar looking scar on his right cheek walked in first. He held his sword out in front of him and walked cautiously toward Samson.

"I remember you," Samson laughed. "You're the little fool who killed my father. I guess I shouldn't have let you live after all." He swung to knock the blade from the man's hand, but the soldier struck first and threw him off balance. In one fluid motion, Samson was pinned face-down onto the ground. He tried to struggle free, but the soldier held him firmly in place.

"Let me see this great Samson," a finely dressed man said as he walked confidently into the house followed by his four cronies. He knelt down in front of the shaved Israelite and roughly turned his face so he could look at him. He was small and round, and his breath in Samson's face smelled like overripe fruit. He laughed and spit on Samson's bald head. "You're nothing!" he said as his fat belly shook with laughter. Samson tried to struggle, but the scarred soldier on his back pulled his arm into an impossible position, sending a searing pain into his shoulder.

The fat Philistine lord walked over to Delilah and kissed her solidly on the mouth. "You've done very well, my dear," he said as he wiped the moisture from his lips. "I have a cartful of silver coins outside your door that you definitely have earned. All five of us have brought you eleven hundred pieces of silver as promised. You'll never have to work again, my beauty." He laughed and fondled her hair, making her shift nervously.

"What are you going to do to him?" she asked, looking slightly sorry for what she had done.

"Well, we'll start by gouging out his eyes," the fat man threw his head back and laughed as though he had just told the funniest joke in the world. "I'm sure you would love to have this honor," he said to the soldier who was holding Samson to the floor. "After what this dog did to you, how he shamed you and your family, you deserve the right to get even." The Philistine lord took a cruel looking iron utensil from his girdle and handed it to the soldier. "This should do just fine." Then he chuckled.

The soldier held the spoonlike instrument in one hand and Samson's face with the other. Four more soldiers joined him and held Samson's arms and legs securely to the ground. Samson tried to fight, but he had no strength left. He finally realized that his God, Yahweh, had been pushed away at last.

CHAPTER 60

Samson sat up with a start. He tried to shake away the darkness, but he soon realized that light no longer existed for him. He cautiously brought his hands up to his face and felt his rough, stubbled cheeks and the swollen, empty holes that once held his eyes. He was dripping in a sweat that had washed away his fever and with it his dreams of the past.

He felt the straw on the ground around him and decided he must still be in a barn of some type. The salt in the air and the distant sound of sea birds told him he was somewhere along the shores of the Great Sea. Slowly, he started to put the pieces together—Delilah's betrayal, the soldier who took his eyes, the long painful journey through Philistine towns. His head throbbed, and he wished he could go back to sleep. Holding his knees against his chest like a child, he rocked back and forth and moaned. Here he was, the great Samson, the deliverer of the Israelites, bald and blind and helpless. After every rebellious thing he had done, God finally had given up on him. *How could I have allowed this to happen? Why did I tell Delilah the secret of my strength? Did I really believe that I had done everything on my own, that God's covenant had nothing to do with all of my victories?* Yes, he had broken his Nazirite vow before, and he had been able to recover quickly—but this was different. His hair was the last sure sign that he was set apart for something special, and he had let that woman take it from him! The pounding in his head was forgotten as a deep, soul-wrenching pain in his heart took its place.

"Oh, God, what have I done?" he whispered up into the blackness above him. "Just kill me now. I don't deserve to live." His shoulders heaved as he sobbed, but there were no tears left. The Philistines had taken those along with his eyes. He didn't hear the movement of the Philistines at the door.

"He's awake." It was the voice of the woman who had been caring for him.

"Good. Give him something to eat, and let's get going. I'm sure our people in Gaza are eager to see the great Samson," another somehow familiar voice replied.

Samson heard soft footsteps come toward him. A small hand took his and placed a piece of bread in it. "You'd better eat this. You'll need your strength," she said in her Philistine accent. "Can you walk?"

"Get away from him," a man called roughly. "Your services are no longer needed. Someone pay her and get her out of here." A soldier grabbed Samson under both arms and lifted him to his feet. "Get up, you dog!" the soldier hissed in his face as he tried to lift him.

Samson collapsed back onto the hay in response.

"I can't carry him to the horse by myself," the soldier called. "Get a couple men in here to help me."

More hands, more jostling. Finally, Samson was placed back onto a horse. This time he was able to sit up instead of being flung like a sack over the back of the animal. He remembered how much he hated riding horses as he clung to the mane and held on. On they walked. Samson could smell the sea and feel a breeze always coming from his right, so they must have been headed south. Gaza. That's what the soldiers had said. They were going to Gaza. They were the people who had killed his cousin Joel. They were the ones who had come out to fight him at the Rock of Etam. They had tried to trap him inside their city gates. The memories of his victories over them in the past seemed like a faraway dream or a story he had heard once as a child. It couldn't have been he who had pulled the gates out of the ground. He couldn't have killed a thousand men with only the jawbone of a donkey. It wasn't real. The only thing that was real was the pain, darkness, and shame that surrounded him right now.

He slumped forward on the horse, almost falling off more than once. *Why won't God just let me die?*

CHAPTER 61

"You're almost to your new home, Samson," a man riding next to him snickered. "Look, the new gates are even better than the old ones that you destroyed. Oh, that's right, you can't see them." Several men nearby laughed.

"Get him off that horse!" another man shouted. "He's not going to ride into Gaza like a hero. We'll drag him if we have to."

The caravan stopped, and Samson was pulled to the ground. He lay there for a moment, thinking that if he didn't get up, they would have to kill him. Instead, they tied him to a horse and pulled him through the dirt as promised. Eventually, Samson was able to get to his feet. He stumbled, but would not allow himself to fall again. He may be defeated, he may be blind, but he was not going to allow them to drag him through the streets of a city inhabited by God's enemy.

Samson could feel the air getting thicker as they entered the city. People shouted and jeered as he walked through the crowds.

"Where's your great God now, mighty Samson?" one man shouted from a safe distance.

He didn't hear the other barbs—that was the only one that stuck. He realized at that moment that he had shamed not only himself; he had shamed the God of Israel. Though he had taken the credit for all his great victories in the past, it really wasn't he who had defeated the Philistines—it was Yahweh. Now that he had allowed himself to be stripped of all dignity and strength, he was making God look weak. He couldn't help but laugh bitterly to himself. He had been so blind until now. Now, without his eyes, he could finally see clearly—none of his feats of strength had been about him!

In spite of the pain, Samson stood straighter and tried to walk with his head held high. Even in his hour of defeat, he had to represent his God with as much dignity as possible. He tuned out the insults and inwardly turned to the God of his fathers. *I'm so sorry*, he silently prayed. *I've let You down, and I've let all Your faithful followers down. I can't expect You to forgive me for my pride and arrogance, but please, don't forget Your people. There are so many in Israel who still worship You faithfully. I saw them in Shiloh. They need You. I know You tried to use me and I failed, but please don't abandon them. Don't allow these heathens to destroy those who love You.*

While he silently talked to God, the rest of the world disappeared. He felt a peace and comfort wash over him, and for the first time since leaving the Sorek Valley, he had hope. He remembered the stories of his childhood—Abraham and his weak faith when God promised him a son, Joseph and his arrogance toward his brothers, Moses and his impatience. God had not abandoned His people before, even after they made mistakes. Somehow he had a feeling God would work things out.

After being paraded through the streets of Gaza, Samson was taken to a small, musty-smelling building. He was pushed onto the ground and untied.

"This is your new home," a strange voice explained. "Get some sleep. You have a big day tomorrow."

"What are you going to do to me? Are you going to execute me?" he asked without fear.

The man laughed. "No, you're not getting off that easy. Not after everything you've done to us. No, we're going to put that big strong body of yours to work grinding wheat. It's the least you can do to repay us for all the damage you've done to our cities over the years. After the wheat harvest, who knows."

Samson felt cold shackles placed on his wrists and ankles.

"We're not taking any chances," the guard explained. "And don't even think about trying to escape. Half our army is stationed outside this prison. If you try anything, they'll make sure you're sorry for it."

Samson had no intention of fighting them. He could barely stand on his own legs; how was he supposed to escape heavy bronze shackles and guards? Maybe the old Samson, but that man was gone.

The guard left, and Samson leaned his head against the cold stone wall. He drew his knees to his chest to try to fight off the chill. He missed his bed in Zorah with the warm blankets and sweet smelling food. He knew his family would be back from Shiloh. They were sure to have heard what had happened to him. News like that always spread fast. He was sorry for the pain he was certainly causing his mother. His body trembled with cold.

"Here," a voice nearby startled him. "You can use my blanket until you warm up." Someone tossed something rough and damp on top of him. The smell almost made him gag, but he recovered and smoothed the rag over his body.

"Thank you."

"You're Samson from Zorah, right?" the man asked as he sat down next to him.

"I was."

"My name is Jachin. My family used to live just outside of Bethlehem."

"Yes, I've been to Bethlehem several times," Samson replied, thankful to have a fellow Israelite nearby.

"I know. I remember seeing you years ago at a feast. Of course you looked much different with your hair . . ." His voice trailed off. "I'm sorry. I haven't talked to anyone in a very long time. I guess I'm a little out of practice."

"How long have you been here?" Samson asked.

"I don't know. At first, I tried marking the days on the wall, but then I lost track. I've been here for at least five wheat harvests; that much I know for sure. They use me for planting and grinding. That's probably what they'll have you do since you're big like me. It's really not so bad. As long as you keep moving, they won't beat you too badly."

"Are there others here?" Samson said when he heard movement coming from the corners.

"Yes, there are six of us right now, counting you. I've seen many others come and go in the years since I've been here. Not many men are built to work on a threshing floor for such long hours. Most of them just give up and die. But I'm sure you'll do fine," he added quickly. "I'm sure you're stronger than most, even now."

"Shut up, Jachin," a voice from the corner called. "We're trying to sleep. Leave the poor man alone. He's been through enough already."

"Don't mind him," Jachin whispered. "That's Abihu from Debir; he's not very friendly. And over there you have Elam, Terah, and Gehazi, but you'll meet them in the morning."

"Thank you for the blanket, Jachin. I'm warm enough now if you want to take it back."

"No," he replied, covering Samson's feet with the rag. "I want you to use it tonight. It's . . . well, it's a real honor to be able to share it with you." Jachin seemed suddenly speechless.

Samson slid down and tried to find a comfortable position for sleep. "Thank you, Jachin. I'm glad I know you."

The man took Samson's hand and kissed it as he would a king. "No. Thank *you*. You have no idea how much hope you've given me in my lifetime. Well, good night."

Samson couldn't believe this man would still treat him with such respect, even now that he had been stripped of all dignity. How could he inspire hope in anyone in this state? But then he remembered, it wasn't him—it was God. Maybe this weak vessel could still be used to help his people.

CHAPTER 62

Early the next morning, Samson woke to rough hands pulling him to his feet. Someone threw cold water on him, causing him to sputter and cough.

"Wake up, sunshine!" one of the guards called out as his friends laughed. "It's time for you filthy Hebrews to get to work."

Someone forced his mouth open and shoved a piece of moldy bread between his teeth. "Eat your breakfast. You won't get anything else until tonight."

Samson tried not to vomit as he chewed the moldy bread. He quickly washed it down with the water that was placed in his hand. Before he was finished drinking, one of the guards pulled on the chain connected to his wrist. The cup in his hand fell to the floor with a clang. The guards roared with laughter.

"OK, that's enough," someone spoke from the door. "Get these men to the threshing floor. They've got work to do."

The chains on Samson's arms and legs were yanked by several men, causing him to struggle awkwardly to keep his balance. He fell once and the soldiers laughed and kicked him until he stood up. *I must try to keep moving*, he vowed silently.

After a short walk, he was taken into what must have been the threshing room. It smelled as though it was close to the sea, with a comfortable breeze blowing through that would help separate the heavy grain from the lighter chaff when it was time to begin winnowing. He had never participated in threshing wheat, but he had seen it done a few times during his travels. It was usually done by the lowest members of society, which explained why Samson was given the undesirable task now.

"Get moving!" someone shouted. The chains were left on his wrists and ankles, and he was pushed up against the handle that turned the upper millstone. It took Samson several rotations of the floor to get a feel for the space. It seemed to be a large circular area enclosed by a low stone wall of some kind. Another prisoner was assigned to funnel the grain into a cone-shaped hole in the upper stone. The flour produced between the stones was collected on a cloth surrounding the lower stone. Whenever Samson stopped to rest, he felt the sharp sting of a whip on his bare back.

He thought about all kinds of things while he was turning the millstone. He wondered what had happened to the beautiful clothes that Delilah had made for him. He wondered if all the money she received for betraying him was enough to satisfy her. He remembered the fat Philistine lord who had kissed her, and he wondered what kind of relationship they had. *Why was I such a fool when it came to women? Perhaps if I had listened to my parents and married a nice Israelite girl, none of this would have happened. Perhaps if I had been less distracted, I would have been able to do more to deliver the Israelites from the Philistines.* Well, it didn't matter now. He just had to keep moving. All he could do now was walk in circles grinding grain until the day his enemies finally decided to let him die.

Day after day, it was the same thing. Early in the morning he was taken to the mill, where he walked in circles until he felt like he was going to collapse. One of the men who slept in his cell died sometime during the hottest part of the summer. He was quickly replaced with someone else. In the evenings, the prisoners were so tired they didn't have energy to do much more than eat the putrid food that was thrown at them before falling to the floor in exhaustion. Only Jachin seemed to feel much like talking. Samson found his chatter comforting, though he was usually too tired to respond. Sometimes the man talked to him about his family. They were also shepherds, but they lived in rocky caves and traveled whenever they needed to find greener pasture. Jachin explained how his family had been stopped on the road one day by Philistine soldiers. They abused his mother and younger sister while he sat helplessly nearby with a sword at his throat. The entire family, along with their flock, was then seized by the soldiers. He was brought to Gaza to work; the rest of them were scattered into the wind like the chaff over the threshing floor. He told the story with absolutely no emotion in his voice, which was sadder to Samson than if the man had cried out his tale in a flood of tears.

Before falling asleep at night, Jachin held his musty blanket over his head, knelt in a corner, and prayed. Sometimes Samson would hear him whispering his pleas to God long after everyone else was asleep. One night, Samson crawled over to join him. The two men prayed, and then whispered the words of a song they had both learned as children. Jachin recited stories he had memorized about Joseph during his time in prison and Moses leading the enslaved Israelites to freedom. The time of worship filled Samson with peace and hope. He had been a Nazirite his entire life, but he had never had a relationship with the real Yahweh—the loving God who formed man from the dust of the earth and breathed life into his nostrils. This new love filled him until he thought he would burst with it. He had never felt this kind of love in the arms of a Philistine woman. Night after night, as tired as he was, he never missed the opportunity to worship with his friend Jachin.

When the threshing was finished, Samson wondered what the Philistines would have him do next. He didn't have to wonder long.

CHAPTER 63

Early one morning a guard came in and shook Samson awake. "It's time to go," he said as he pulled Samson to his feet.

"The threshing is finished. Where are you taking him?" Jachin spoke from a corner.

"Mind your own business, dog!" the Philistine shouted. "Samson has been summoned by the Lord Maoch. He gets to meet Dagon today."

Samson stood up and adjusted the loincloth that was now his only piece of clothing. "I've met your god Dagon, and I wasn't impressed," he commented.

The guard answered with a hard punch in the gut. "You won't be smiling when Dagon takes you as a sacrifice," he said as he jerked the chains on Samson's arms and led him away from the prison.

"May Yahweh bless you, Samson!" Jachin called boldly.

"He already has, my friend," Samson replied.

The guard led Samson through the streets of town, but only a few people were out this early in the morning. When they reached their destination, Samson recognized the smell of burning incense. He remembered the feeling of the cold stone under his feet. He was in Dagon's temple once again. He was taken down a corridor off the main part of the temple to a small room, probably like the one he had stayed in with the prostitute. The guard seated him and handed him a rag and slid a large basin of water in front of him. He was told to wash and then he was left alone. It was the first time in months that he was given an opportunity to clean himself. He started with his face, taking care around the empty holes that once held his eyes. He then washed the top of his head where his hair was beginning to grow back. He felt his short beard and couldn't help but smile at the familiar feeling of the hair on his chin. It reminded him that God didn't change and that His love endured in spite of humanity's mistakes. Just as the rains follow droughts and the crops grow and ripen in their seasons, God would continue to renew His people every time they stumbled.

He quickly finished washing then sat against a cold wall and waited for whatever was to come. He no longer had his great strength, but he didn't need it anymore. He knew God's strength was enough to support him against any foe he had to face—even Dagon himself.

A short time later, the door opened, and Samson could hear several people enter the room.

Someone knelt right in front of him and grabbed his beard. The rough hand moved his head around, examining him closely. Samson recognized the smell of overripe fruit and knew it was the Philistine lord who had paid Delilah for his capture.

"You must be Lord Maoch," Samson said with more boldness than he had used since leaving the Sorek Valley.

"That's right. I see you're still very sharp, even without your eyes."

"I don't need my eyes. I could smell your filth from across the room."

Someone gave him a sharp kick in the side, but he sensed that it didn't come from the round little man who called himself a lord.

"I'd like you to meet the other lords," Maoch said as he stood and walked away from Samson. "It took some time to get everyone assembled, but the rulers of all five of the Philistine cities have come to see you today," Maoch said as he walked back and forth in the now crowded room. "We also have another special guest who has played a very important role in your capture." At first Samson thought they had brought in Delilah, but he realized it was a man standing in front of him. The man didn't speak, but eventually knelt down in front of him to get a better look.

"It's hard to believe you've come to this, Samson." From the voice he recognized his cousin Alvah!

Samson clenched his fists as the flood of memories came washing over him. "What are you doing here?" he growled.

"Don't you know? I live here now. I had to leave Timnah after they killed my wife, Peles."

"She was my wife," Samson interrupted.

"Yes, well, none of that matters now, does it? She's dead and you're nothing but a disgusting shell of what you once were." He stood up and walked back to the lords. "I guess I'm the only one left standing, aren't I?" he said smugly.

"Yes, and if it wasn't for our good friend Alvah here, we might never have been able to find your family's home in Zorah or to discover your weakness for the fairer sex," Lord Maoch taunted. "Now, dear Samson, we have a big day planned. First, entertainment, then, our big harvest sacrifice to Dagon. And you will provide both for us." The putrid-smelling lord was back in his face, making Samson want to gag.

"I don't care what you do to me, Maoch."

"That's Lord Maoch!" the man hissed in his face.

"As I was saying, *Lord* Maoch," Samson replied defiantly, "you can do to me whatever you like. My God Yahweh, the true God of heaven, will deal with you and your little statue Dagon."

Samson was showered with kicks and punches from the men standing over him. He just shielded his head and took the blows without even trying to get to his feet.

"That's enough," Maoch shouted. "He's no good to us if you kill him now!"

Two soldiers picked Samson up off the ground. He moaned with the effort it took to stand after the beating he had just received. Someone threw the remaining water from the basin in his face to keep him from passing out.

Several soldiers pulled him out of the room by his chains and led him limping painfully back down the corridor into the temple. Even before the door was opened, he could hear the crowds gathered inside.

"Stop here," Maoch commanded. "I don't want all of you soldiers taking Samson in as though he were some kind of mighty hostage. Get my son! He will take Samson in like a big, tame dog."

Several men nearby agreed and snickered at the thought of the great Samson being held by a child.

Moments later, a young boy was put in front of Samson. He wasn't even strong enough to carry the chains on Samson's wrists, so instead the boy was given his hand.

"This is him?" the little boy exclaimed as he examined the captive. "Well, he's nothing but a big, ugly animal. Their god must be pretty dumb to use *him* as a deliverer!" The men thought this was hysterical, and they laughed as though it was the funniest thing they had ever heard. Samson felt the old familiar anger burn in the pit of his stomach. If only he had his strength back, he would silence their laughter forever.

The door to the temple was opened, and Maoch's mouthy son led Samson into the center of the large auditorium. Shouts erupted from the crowd gathered there when they saw the prisoner. From the noise, Samson guessed there had to be thousands of people filling both the upper and lower levels of the temple. Objects were thrown at him from above, and insults were hurled at him from every direction. Samson simply stood still in the center of the crowd, holding his head up with as much dignity as he could manage.

"Ladies and gentlemen," Lord Maoch called out, trying to quiet the crowd. "Can I have your attention?" Finally the ruckus died down enough so he could be heard.

"You see before you today the great Samson—deliverer of the Israelites." The crowd exploded with laughter.

"This animal you see here has tried to destroy our country. He is the enemy of our god Dagon. But as you can see, he's nothing! His god—the so-called God of heaven—is nothing!" The crowd cheered wildly, and Maoch waited for them to quiet before he continued. "Dagon has delivered our enemy into our hands."

Samson was confused and disoriented by the noise that followed. Someone came up from behind him and pushed him to the ground. The crowd laughed and cheered. He felt the foot of the little boy on his back. He rolled over and stood up shakily, only to be knocked down again. When he stood back up, he tried to back away from whoever was pushing him, but he walked right into someone else. Again and again, he was shoved and pushed to the ground. The people standing over him kicked him and spit on him. Rotten food was thrown at him from the crowds as people cheered hysterically. He considered staying on the ground, but something inside of him made him get up over and over again. His knees shook and his head throbbed, but he couldn't just lie down and let them insult his God.

"And now, my fellow Philistines, we have a great treat for you." Maoch again quieted the crowd. "Today we will offer Samson as a sacrifice to Dagon. His blood will be an offering to thank Dagon for delivering the Israelites into our hands. With Samson dead, we will destroy the rest of the filthy Hebrews that have been a thorn in our side for generations. We will rid our lands of them and their invisible god!"

The crowd erupted again. Samson's head swam, and he felt as though he might collapse.

"Please," he said to the boy standing next to him, "let me lean against something so I can rest for a moment."

The boy took his hand and led him to two large pillars that were just a little more than shoulder-width apart. He could feel the building vibrate from the people overhead stomping and shouting wildly as they worked themselves into a frenzy.

Samson hung his head, trying to catch his breath, but then he felt something strange but familiar that he hadn't felt in a very long time. Something like a bolt of lightning tingled down his spine. His pulse hammered through his body, drowning out the sound of the crowd. Then he heard a small Voice speaking softly into his ear.

"Samson, push."

He turned his blind eyes toward heaven. "Is that You, Lord?" he whispered.

"It's always been Me, beloved."

"Oh, God," he cried aloud. "Please forgive me for my pride and stupidity!"

"I already have," came the barely audible response.

Samson choked back a sob. "If it pleases You, Lord, use me one more time. Fill me with Your strength again, not for my glory and honor, but so that everyone will know You are the true God of heaven and earth."

Samson felt a soft breeze envelope him that somehow reminded him of the comfort of his mother's arms. "Push," came the whisper on the breeze. "Push."

Samson placed his right hand on one pillar and his left hand on the other. He had no way of knowing how large the stone columns were or that they were the support for the roof, but God knew.

"Push!" the Voice was more urgent this time.

Samson took a deep breath and pushed with every bit of strength he had. He felt the stone crack under his fingers, and he continued to push. At first, the crowd laughed, but then something changed.

"Push."

The columns started giving way, and the second floor of the temple began to crumble and shift. The Philistines' laughter turned to frantic screams as they scrambled to get out of the collapsing building.

"Push."

And that was the last thing Samson heard.

EPILOGUE

God did hear Samson's prayers, as well as the prayers of His people scattered throughout Israel. Samson's mighty strength returned to him, and he was able to bring down the temple of Dagon and crush everyone inside. In that one moment, Samson killed more than three thousand of God's enemies, including the lords and rulers of all five of the major Philistine cities. In his death, Samson killed more Philistines than he had in his entire life.

The news of what happened in Gaza quickly spread throughout the country. Samson's entire family was in Shiloh celebrating the Festival of Tabernacles when the story reached them. They immediately headed south to bring Samson's body home for burial. When his brothers, uncles, and cousins reached Gaza, they walked through the gates without any harassment. They had no trouble finding the ruins of the once great temple. The men of Samson's family searched through the rubble until they found his remains lying under what was left of the two support pillars. Though his hair and beard were short, his eyes were gone, and his body was badly broken, the smile on Samson's lifeless face brought peace to his brothers' hearts.

Samson's remains were taken home, and he was laid to rest in his father's tomb between Zorah and Eshtaol. A crowd of mourners gathered while Eli, the high priest from Shiloh, offered words of courage and hope to his people. He reminded them that God could find strength in weakness and that He would never abandon His people as long as they remained faithful. When he was finished speaking, the hired mourners wailed, and Samson's mother cried softly. Eli brushed away a tear that fell into his now gray beard. A little boy wearing a white robe walked up to Eli and took his hand. The old man looked down at his new apprentice,

Samuel, and smiled. The child filled him with a feeling of hope for the future, hope for his people. Maybe someday this child would find the strength to lead God's people to unity and faithfulness. Eli patted the boy's hand and smiled through his tears. He knew he just needed to have faith. God promised He would deliver them—and God always keeps His promises.

A NOTE TO THE READER

I'm sure you will notice that most of the characters in my story are fictional (or at least the name given to the unknown person mentioned in the Bible is fictional), but the main characters are absolutely real. As you read this book, you may think some of Samson's great feats are just figments of my overactive imagination, but the most unusual and unbelievable acts performed by Samson are straight from the biblical account of his life (see Judges 13–16).

It is my hope and prayer that this book will help readers relate to and understand Samson better. He was deeply flawed and troubled—but aren't we all? He lived in an environment where his promise to God made him an outsider—sound familiar? He made plenty of mistakes. He was prideful and arrogant. He trusted the wrong people, put himself in bad situations, and made terrible choices—but in the end, Samson turned fully back to God.

In Hebrews 11:32, Samson is listed among the great heroes of faith, in the same category as King David and the prophet Samuel. Once again, God shows us that even in our weakness, He can make us strong. We all make mistakes, we all stumble and fall, but Samson teaches us to get back up and push on. I pray that we will all be inspired by Samson's life, and death, to dedicate ourselves completely to our heavenly Father and to finish the work He has asked us to do (see Matthew 28:19, 20).

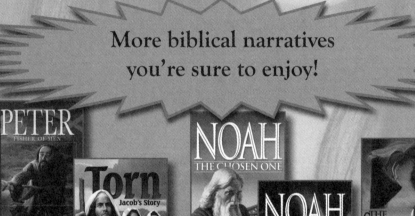

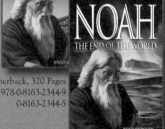

3689318 9 R00166